SANTORINI SUMMER

ESCAPE TO THE ISLANDS

HOLLY GREENE

At the grand old age of thirty-two, Olivia Clarke was beginning to wonder if the best years of her life had already passed her by.

She shut the door of her flat behind her with a sigh after a long day at work. Heading into the kitchen, she tossed her keys on the countertop along with her handbag.

It was Friday night in London, one of the liveliest cities on earth, and she had nowhere to go and nothing to do.

Her fiancé had left and taken Olivia's so-called best friend along with him. She had become so downbeat and disillusioned over the past three months since the two people she'd loved most in the world had run off together, and staying in at weekends had become something of a habit.

She went to the cupboard and pulled out a bottle of white wine. Pouring a generous glass she slumped on the couch, unbuttoning the top two buttons on her grey blouse and piled her long dark hair in a heap on the top of her head, fastening it with a hair bobble.

Was this it? Her life couldn't be over already, could it?

"Ah you have to snap out of this," she chastened herself out loud.

She wasn't entirely sure how to do that though. Her heart ached and her pride stung every time she thought about the horrible end to her wedding plans.

She was in a rut and although no one would blame her after everything that had happened, it still didn't make it right.

Shaking her head, she got up and went to get her phone. Tonight was a takeaway night to be sure.

She ordered some Chinese food and went off to the shower. She knew they would not have the delivery to her until well after she was out of the shower and on her second glass of wine. She had ordered from Hu Hans Restaurant many times before.

Sipping her wine, she went into the bathroom and started the water running. Undressing, she adjusted the temperature then got in and stood there, enjoying the hot water as it ran over her body.

The shower was about the only place she could go to get away from things these days. It was so easy for her to meditate in the mist and shampoo and think of nothing at all.

Once she felt clean and refreshed, Olivia got out and dressed in her red silk pajamas. They were a gift from her aunt Carole, and she loved the feel of them on her skin. It was a little early in the evening for bedtime wear, but what the hell, she wasn't going anywhere.

She finished her first glass of wine and poured the second one. After only a few sips the doorbell rang.

The food was fast tonight, she thought, getting up and going to the door. She tipped the delivery guy and took her food inside, deciding to just eat it out of the box because she was suddenly feeling very hungry.

Sitting on her couch Olivia ate her Mongolian Chicken and spring rolls with gusto, enjoying the flavors. Just spicy enough to get her attention, especially with the plum sauce. The spring rolls were also a special treat she had come to enjoy on her Friday nights in.

When she finished, she sighed with contentment and leaned back on her couch, enjoying the feeling for a time.

Staying home and enjoying a night to herself was not a

bad thing, she reasoned, except she did it every weekend now.

Her friends from work in the accountancy practice had been pushing her to get out more, as had a few family members - Aunt Carole in particular.

Yet Olivia had not been able to find the energy or time.

Now this week, a work thing had gone sideways (another blow to her ego) and she felt more despondent than ever.

Sighing, she filled her glass a third time and her phone rang. Glancing down she saw it was her aunt. She smiled. Talking to Aunt Carole was always nice - the sixty-six-year-old was fun and full of chat and energy. Unlike her miserable niece.

"Hey Carole, how are things?" Olivia said by way of greeting, trying to sound upbeat.

"Great, love. How are you doing? I hope you're out and about enjoying yourself this fine Friday night - what are you up to?"

"Ah you know, same old thing," Olivia answered and took another sip of her wine.

"Chinese or pizza?" her aunt asked, deadpan.

"Uh, Chinese …. how did you know?"

"Friday nights you either have Chinese food or pizza. Saturday is usually Indian, or maybe Korean if you're feeling adventurous," was the response.

Olivia sighed. "You're right, Carole. I have fallen into a rut. I was actually considering going out tonight, but work was awful this week and I thought to hell with it," she responded.

She did not like moaning about her problems to people, but Aunt Carole was an exception. She was never judgmental.

"Ah no. You didn't get the promotion? I thought you were a shoo-in."

"I did too, but they gave it to that twenty-two-year-old newcomer, blond skinny and perky, you know the type," Olivia took a longer drink of her wine in disgust.

"That is ridiculous. You may not be skinny but you are perkier than most. What is their problem?"

Olivia had to laugh at that. It was true that she was more on the voluptuous side. Still, no matter how much they joked, being overlooked had made her feel even more old and past it. She sighed, despite herself.

"Talk to me, honey. I know your life has been hard the last few months but is it something else?" Carole asked.

Maybe it was the wine, but Olivia opened up further. "I suppose I just feel like I'm over the hill, Carole. My fiancé left me for my best friend and my job prospects disappeared in the flash of blond hair and blue eyes. To be honest, I don't have the drive to do much of anything these days. It's depressing and that just makes me want to stay home even more.

I don't know what to do. Will these feelings ever go away? Or am I destined to be a layabout for the rest of my life? I mean the food is good, as well as the wine but..." She trailed off and sighed again.

"First off, stop that line of thinking. You are nowhere near past it and I am going to prove it to you. Would you take my advice, love? Just a couple of small suggestions but I think they will help you in ways you cannot imagine," her aunt told her.

"OK. It is not like I have any great ideas at the moment," Olivia said with another heavy sigh. She realized she was doing way too much sighing lately.

"Good. Now start by getting that miserable ex's number and messages off your phone," was her aunt's first piece of advice. "You don't need to see Derek the Dick's name every time you scroll through your contacts. You don't need to listen to his voice, or read his texts either."

Olivia set her phone down and put Carole on speaker so she could scroll through her contacts and highlight her errant ex. She pressed edit and then delete. The message *"Are you sure?"* came up on the screen and she hesitated.

"Olivia, are you there?" her aunt asked and she realized she had been silent for too long.

"Still here, just doing it now," she told her, but still

Olivia could not bring herself to press the yes command on the phone. Her eyes misted over briefly and she wiped them as her heart ached afresh.

"Okay then. Next, you need to call work and tell them you are going to re-evaluate your position and use up the rest of your current holiday leave. They won't like it, but they need you there and will go along with it, you know they will," Carole said in a cheerful voice.

This distracted Olivia a little from her heartbreak.

"And what am I supposed to do with the time off? I really do need that job you know," she said hesitantly.

"With your qualifications, you could get another in no time at all and they know it. They were probably hoping you would just go along with things. This will let them know they are at risk of losing you. It will also enable you to be on a plane to Greece first thing next week. You know my little timeshare in Santorini?" Carole asked and Olivia nodded, confused. "It's free at the moment and will suit you perfectly. The island is one of the most beautiful places on earth, and at this time of year will be full of people just having fun and enjoying themselves. You deserve to do the same. Use up your holiday time to relax, love. You can have the place for two weeks - my treat," Carole continued, and Olivia felt a lump in her throat at her aunt's generosity.

"Are you sure? I mean, this is too much…" she stammered.

"It's not enough as far as I'm concerned. You know, when your parents passed away the only thing that might be considered good about it was that I got to see you grow from a promising young girl to the proud and capable woman you are today. I am, and have always been, proud of you. I am sure they would be too. So take a break and enjoy yourself, Olivia, you need some fun," she finished.

Feeling a sudden surge of her old determination at her aunt's words, Olivia reached out to tap the "yes" button on her smartphone screen.

In an instant, Derek's name and his texts all disappeared into thin air.

Carole was right. Santorini sounded like heaven. She'd never been there, but over the years had heard Carole rave about her beautiful Greek Island retreat.

Yes, Olivia needed this.

And she was going to try her damnedest to make the most of it.

CHAPTER TWO

First thing Monday morning, Olivia checked the time of her flight on the Departures board at Heathrow Airport.

She had called her boss's mobile the day after speaking with her aunt to let her know that she was taking two weeks holiday leave.

Julia had not been happy, but as Aunt Carole had predicted, she had still okayed the request.

Perhaps the company did want her to stay after all?

Olivia decided for the next two weeks it did not matter; all she needed to do was concentrate on enjoying herself.

She was going on holiday for the first time in years! She took out her iPhone and brought up the Santorini tourist website again.

The pictures were incredible, and looking at them was already melting her cares away. Her honeymoon with Derek was to be in France, but this looked far better.

The little Greek town her aunt's cottage was based in was lit up by lights from cafes and tavernas along the coastline in a dusky sunset shot, and whitewashed buildings with cerulean blue rooftops were bathed in golden light.

The entire area seemed to glow with warmth and in another daytime image, the Aegean Sea looked a heavenly blue. There were sailboats dotted about on the water that immediately made Olivia want to lie back on the deck of one and fall asleep beneath the warm sunshine.

Soon, she reminded herself, *soon you can do that and more.*

While going to such a destination was exciting, it was also a little daunting. She had never taken a trip abroad on her own before.

A flight announcer called her flight number then, and Olivia grabbed her things and stood.

"Here we go…" she whispered.

UNFORTUNATELY FOR OLIVIA, the flight was long and drawn out due to adverse weather over France and then there was a stopover in Athens that lasted for two hours, so the journey from London to Athens ended up taking far more than the anticipated four hours.

When she finally disembarked the plane at Athens airport to pick up her connection to Santorini, she was already exhausted.

Olivia got a strong cappuccino to keep her going before she went and retrieved her bags for the next leg of her trip.

She had packed as lightly as she could, but a two-week stay still required a couple of small suitcases. She retrieved her luggage and stacked it on a little hand cart. Her frustration level was rising with her fatigue and she managed to nab a passing sky car to help her make the connecting flight to Santorini. She had always been self-sufficient but decided enough was enough.

Fortunately, the Greek female airport attendant spoke English and Olivia could explain what she needed.

She almost melted in relief as her bags were loaded on and she was offered a seat. She thanked the woman twice as she sat down.

"You are amazing, thank you so much. I did not expect the flight to take so long. There were storms…" She trailed off and the woman kept smiling and Olivia could read the sympathy in her eyes. "I just hope I don't miss my connection."

"My pleasure Madam, it is my job and my desire to

help you get where you need to go. Just sit back and relax now," the Greek woman said and got in to drive the cart.

In moments Olivia was on her way.

"I am Olivia, by the way. May have your name?" She had completely missed the lovely woman's name tag and was feeling flustered. She felt terrible.

"I am Alkippe, Madam. Thank you for asking. Are you going to be in Santorini for very long?" the attendant asked as she weaved them through the crowded terminal.

"Two weeks. Although it feels like it's already taken two weeks just getting this far," she joked and sipped her coffee. Fortunately, it was still warm but also very strong. They knew how to do coffee here, that was for sure.

Alkippe laughed softly. "I know travelling can some-times feel that way. I am sure that once you get to the island all your cares will wash away. I have an old uncle who lives in Fira and I have spent much time there. It will be enjoyable for you, I am sure," she said encouraging.

Olivia smiled a little at the woman's sincerity, appreciating her effort.

"I am sure you are right. My aunt recommended Santorini as the perfect place to sort myself out, and she is never wrong about these things."

Alkippe laughed again. "Aunts and Uncles Madam, they are always right. If they someday are not, we will just not mention it," she joked.

Olivia laughed and before she knew it she was at her departure gate. Between her coffee and Alkippe, she was feeling much better, and able to face the last leg of her trip.

"Thank you again for all your help," she told her, once her luggage was unloaded. She gave her a generous tip and Alkippe continued to smile.

"I am glad to have helped, Madam. Enjoy your time and I hope you have a wonderful trip!" she told her. Then the Greek woman climbed back onto the cart and was off to save someone else.

The friendly chat had been nice and helped Olivia feel not so mussed and dirty after her long and tiring first leg. She finished her coffee just in time to board the little plane to Santorini with the other passengers.

The plane was packed to capacity and Olivia realised she was hitting the Greek Islands in peak summer tourist season.

The thought bothered her at first, but then watching the excitement of her fellow travellers she began to relax and be happy that she would not be alone, and that there would be others striving for some kind of peace and fun, the same as she was. At least that was what she told herself as they soared over mainland Greece.

Even if they hadn't been through what she had,

everyone had something they needed to escape from, didn't they?

CHAPTER THREE

The first thing Olivia did at Santorini airport was get something to eat and another coffee. The falafel was spectacular and the second coffee was even better than the one at Athens.

Then she roused herself to push her luggage cart out front and got a cab. The driver seemed nice, if a little uncommunicative, once Olivia had given him the piece of paper with her aunt's timeshare address on it.

But at this point, she was grateful for the silence.

Olivia sat in the back as they drove away and her jaw just about dropped to the floor as they travelled along a road next to the clear blue Aegean Sea.

The contrast of the crystal clear water, whitewashed buildings and dark volcanic rock was a treat to the eyes.

She unrolled the windows a little and the smell of the salty sea was immediately intoxicating.

She had two weeks to spend in this incredible atmosphere and now that she was here, experiencing it, Olivia smiled to herself and chuckled softly.

Take that, Derek, she thought. He would be amazed to see her now.

She knew her ex had fully expected her to collapse in a heap after losing the likes of him - which she had for a while. But no more. She already had a feeling this place was finally going to help heal her broken heart.

The pain in her gut when she thought of him already seemed lessened.

THE LAST PART of the drive wound through thin streets of what looked like a pretty little fishing village, and Olivia looked up at the buildings they passed. All looked similar and very familiar: whitewashed paint and redbrick trim, with distinctive painted blue domed rooftops and awash with tumbling pink bougainvillaea.

Quintessentially Greek, she thought, admiring the look and feel of her surroundings.

Eventually, the cab driver pulled up to the little white-washed cottage that was to be Olivia's home for the next two weeks, and helped her take her bags to the blue-painted front door.

She thanked him and tipped, waving as he left. Then she went up the small stone path, dragging her suitcases behind her.

Carole had told her that this was a cosy two-bed cottage, and it would be more than enough.

As soon as Olivia turned the key and entered the main room, she dropped her suitcases and walked to the picture window along the back of the house, her mouth open in awe.

The little town seemed to slope downward to the Aegean in a blanket of blue domed roofs and flowers, and from the veranda, the cottage had an unobscured view of a giant central lagoon surrounded by three hundred metre high cliffs with a dormant volcano silhouetted in the distance.

It was quite simply, breathtaking.

Olivia slid open the glass doors and stepped out onto her balcony with a big smile and a laugh from deep inside. The smell of the air and the sight of white sails on amazingly blue water was intoxicating, and she just stood there for a moment, taking it all in.

She walked up to the railing of her little veranda and saw a stone pathway leading down to the coastline, where little cafes and tavernas were dotted along a beachside walkway.

"Thank you, Carole," she whispered softly.

This was perfect.

After everything that had happened, the fact that she was here in this incredible place with stunning coastal views that were already good for the soul, would have seemed like a joke a week earlier.

Now Olivia was laughing with joy.

Something told her it was all going to be all right, that here in Santorini, she would be OK.

CHAPTER FOUR

*L*ater that evening, Olivia waded out of the Aegean Sea feeling exhilarated and relaxed.

Swimming in the warm waters was a treat that she could get used to.

She pushed her hair back from her face and walked through the dark volcanic sand up to where she had left her stuff.

Just up from the beach, there was a patch of yellowish-white grass and a small group of palm trees with hammocks. She had already claimed one of them, and they even had little tables alongside each one for drinks and snacks.

Olivia took a long swallow of the pina colada she had waiting and sighed.

It was a very different sigh to the ones she'd been

releasing since her wedding was cancelled. This was a sigh of pure contentment.

The angle of the hammock afforded her a hypnotic view of the water and coastline so she made herself comfortable.

It was a while yet before she would want dinner, so lying back and watching the world go by seemed like a fantastic idea.

The hammock swung gently, and the breeze off the water was heavenly as it ran over her bare arms and legs.

She was wearing a blue one-piece that was modest yet complimentary to her curves. She had brought a bikini too but was not quite confident enough to try that one out yet. It wasn't that she was overweight or that her belly wasn't flat it was just…she hadn't quite got her confidence back, that was all.

She reached over for the cocktail and drained the glass, before setting the empty container back on the little wood table, then put her sunglasses on.

It was so nice to just relax.

She had absolutely nothing to do, or any place to be, and for one of the first times in her life, Olivia did not mind. She didn't *need* to have something to do every second of every day, not anymore anyway, and definitely not for the next two weeks.

She closed her eyes and could hear the sound of children's voices laughing down by the water, and she smiled lazily. The sound of the surf, distant voices and the slight breeze took her to sleep in no time.

When Olivia awoke, she was startled and sat up. The movement of the hammock reminded her where she was, and she avoided flipping out of it at the last minute.

She realised she had slept the early evening away and the sunset was now in full bloom on the horizon, so she remained in the hammock watching the array of colours slowly change into dusk in front of her.

The Santorini sunset was breathtaking and a reminder that natural beauty trumped all else every time.

She waited until the sun had finally disappeared, and then she got up and stretched, gathered her things and headed back to the cottage to change for the evening.

She wasn't sure what she was going to do exactly, but felt excited about her first night on holiday, and vowed to enjoy every minute.

An hour or so later, Olivia was strolling down the beach to the string of beachside tavernas and cafes she'd seen from the balcony.

She entered the first one she came to, trusting chance. While waiting to be seated she gave herself a quick once over in the mirror behind the bar.

She had dressed in a red halter top and a white mid-length skirt. Her hair was in a ponytail and a few strands had come loose in the ocean breeze and hung around her heart-shaped face.

She was smiling and enjoying the natural lack of effort it took to do so. She used to always smile, but Derek had taken that away from her and she was glad to feel she could still do it.

She followed the Greek waiter who beckoned her to a little round table facing the water. It was one of the last unoccupied tables in the taverna, probably she thought, because it was so small and most people were in groups, enjoying the nightlife.

Olivia was quite happy this first night though, to be an observer.

A black-haired woman in a white blouse and skirt came over to take her order. Olivia was hungry and quickly ordered moussaka and some bread she had seen on another table as an appetiser.

The bread was delivered with hummus; the best she had ever tasted and seemed to compliment the wine the waiter had recommended.

Olivia sat back, watching couples walking past on the beach and felt a stirring in her chest.

That could have been her if her ex had not been such an ass.

She pushed that thought away. No more thinking of Derek the Dick as her aunt had so amusingly monikered him. He had no place in her relaxation time here, she told herself firmly.

It was still difficult though, surrounded as she was by romance and laughter. When her salad arrived, she dug in and found it to be as good as everything else so far. As she ate she continued to observe those around her and decided there were different kinds of romance.

Certainly, there was the romance of couples in love, but there was also the romance of a new place, exotic and exciting. A beautiful night in an idyllic location by the beach surrounded by happy people was also a romantic setting in and of itself, and Olivia did not need to be with anyone to make it so.

She felt her smile return with that realisation, and finishing her salad she leaned back in her chair, sipping her wine. As she did, she felt someone bump into her chair from behind and she turned her head, looking back.

"Oh, I am so sorry. It is getting a little crowded. I didn't mean to bump into you. No harm done I hope?" asked the tremendously handsome man Olivia was looking back at.

The attractive Greek had black swept-back hair and was wearing an open linen shirt. His bare chest was muscular and toned and his face was the chiselled sort beloved by romance writers.

Olivia smiled. "Not at all. It is getting busy, so no worries," she assured him.

"Glad to hear it. I need to catch up with my friends now, but maybe I will see you around?" he said with a hopeful note in his tone.

Olivia was not in any way looking to hook up with anyone, but she appreciated his subtle offer, not to mention appreciative glances. It was a welcome boost to her confidence.

"Sure. Enjoy your evening," she told him.

"You too," he said and went out onto the beach with a last glance over his shoulder at her.

Olivia chuckled to herself, delighted by this unexpected interaction. Maybe she wasn't so past it after all …

"Excuse me, ma'am," said the waitress who had just then showed up to remove her dishes. "Would you like dessert?"

Olivia nodded in a sudden decision. "You know, I would. I was thinking of the Sfakianopita, do you have that here?" she asked.

"Ah yes, ma'am. It is a favourite of our patrons as well as the staff. I will bring you a serving immediately," she said and was off with a smile.

Olivia had heard of the famed Greek dessert and wanted to try it. Sfakianopita was a type of cheese pie with nuts and honey. Just thinking about it made her mouth water despite the big salad she had just eaten.

When it came she was not disappointed. It was decadent, delightful and just what she needed to end her busy day. She sipped the strong coffee that had come with the dessert and decided that, for her first day, she'd done enough.

It had been a long day, she was stuffed, had a little buzz on from her wine, and was ready for sleep.

Olivia paid her bill, including a hefty tip for the lovely staff and walked back along the coastline.

She was waved to by several people she had seen throughout the afternoon near the hammocks, as well as the handsome Greek who had bumped into her table. He was with a group of young people drinking down by the water. Everyone was having a great time and did not appear to have a care in the world.

She left the blinds open on her bedroom window and climbed into the bed, stretching out. It felt heavenly and she could see flashes of light from the village below, along with little glimpses of stars out the window.

What a wonderful, magical place.

Olivia went to sleep with that relaxing thought in her mind and had her first deep, uninterrupted sleep in a very long time.

CHAPTER FIVE

*B*en Norton growled an obscenity when he saw the text from his agent. It simply said *'Call me'* and he knew straight away what *that* was about.

He had barely three months to get his next book to his publishers and he had not written a word. He was well and truly blocked and not a happy man.

Ben did believe in facing things head-on though, so he called Kimberly straight back.

"Might as well get it over with," he muttered to himself as the phone rang.

"Well, there you are, Ben. How is it coming?" his agent asked, and he knew she was not asking about his well-being. That was not her style.

Kimberly was all business. So he decided to be the same.

"Crappy, I have nothing yet, sorry - I am trying," he told her.

"I know, I know. I had a feeling that you might be blocked …" Ben winced at her words. No writer liked to hear that. "…so I went ahead and did you a great big favour - you can repay me later," she added and he was immediately suspicious.

"What kind of favour?"

"I reserved my family's time-share in Santorini, Greece for the next two weeks. It will be the perfect place for you to recharge and maybe get some inspiration. You know the guys at Herod are asking me all the time when the new script is coming, so I figured this might help us both," she said, referring to his publishers.

Ben had a brief notion of turning her down. Just because he was blocked did not mean he wanted to hear it or receive sympathy about it. The moment passed however when he realised this may be exactly what he needed.

The only thing he hated more than being reminded he was blocked, was actually being blocked.

Nice scenery, good weather, and solitude might be just what the doctor ordered. Besides New York could be hell in the summertime.

"I must admit, it sounds pretty good, Kim, and you are right, I will owe you," he told her.

There was a long pause.

"Really? I thought I was going to have to bully you into it! No one likes it when I have to do that, but you know I can," she said and Ben laughed, suddenly feeling some tension release.

"Oh I know; it is why I gave in so fast. When do I leave?"

"Is Thursday good for you? I will e-mail you the details and flight info etc. Two weeks of uninterrupted Greek sunshine, food, wine and hopefully for both our sakes … inspiration."

Ben hoped for the same himself.

LATER THAT SAME WEEK, Ben sipped champagne on the first-class flight the agency had booked for him.

He was an hour out from Athens and he had had a good nap along the way. The food had been passable but the drink was excellent, he thought, as he took another sip.

He had been recognised by a flight attendant an hour into the flight. She apparently had read everything he had written and loved every word.

Ben had a hard time believing those things when he was told.

Looking back, some of his earlier stuff was definitely subpar and he had been lucky to get it published. That did not mean that he did not accept the compliment or sign the copy she was reading of *Surrogate Damage,* his previous novel.

He had written a personalised thank you for her care on the flight. She had been ecstatic and suddenly he was getting even better service than before.

She did ask if he was working on anything new, obviously trying to get a scoop on his upcoming book. Ben did not feel like telling her the truth about his progress so he had hedged.

"I am kicking around a few things, outlining a few ideas. Mostly I am on vacation," he had told her smiling.

Half-truths at best. Ben felt a little guilty, but not too much.

As a heavy reader himself, he never felt it necessary to get all bent out of shape when his favourite authors did not produce as fast as he would prefer.

Then again, as a writer too, he knew the difficulties and dangers of rushing things. That thought reminded him he was pretty much in a position to rush things himself and that brought his mind back to the problem at hand.

It was just that nothing seemed interesting to him

lately, not enough to write about anyway. He had fallen into a rut creatively and had to find a way to climb out.

Maybe this little jaunt to Santorini would be a good start.

CHAPTER SIX

*W*hen he landed in Athens, he said goodbye to the flight attendant and went to get his bags.

It was the middle of the night in Europe and he wanted nothing more at that point than to fly on to Santorini and get some sleep.

He ran into a problem, however.

They could not find his luggage. It was logged into the system as having made it onto the flight, but they just could not find it in Athens.

Ben spent the next three hours waiting and pacing. He drank some coffee and paced some more before they found it. There were many apologies and promises of upgrades and free-flying miles but Ben just waved them off.

All he wanted was to get to his lodgings and hit the hay.

When he got to the departure gate for the little plane that would take him from Athens to Santorini he found he had another hour wait for the next one. He had missed the last flight by ten minutes.

More coffee and surfing the net on his phone ate up the time it took to get on board the connecting flight and be on his way.

By the time they reached the island, the sun was rising and Ben was famished. His frustration level had peaked with how his trip was going so far.

If this was any way like the way the rest of it was going to go, he was beginning to think he should have stayed at home.

Ben went to a café at the airport for breakfast and was greatly relieved by how good the food was at least. Eggs, sausage with a special goat cheese that was wonderful, and the freshest orange juice he had ever tasted.

Once he had eaten his fill, his frustration level had gone back down a little and he reminded himself that was always the way. When he got hungry he got annoyed.

So, he thought cheerfully, I just need to keep myself well-fed.

According to his information, there were lots of bars

and eateries near the house he was staying at, so that would not be a problem.

Outside the terminal, he hailed a cab and loaded his baggage with the knowledge it should be smooth sailing from here on in.

THE TRIP to his lodging was a beautiful tour given by a silent cab driver which was nice. Coming from New York, Ben was used to chatty drivers.

He appreciated the quiet to admire the views and the beautiful village he was being driven through. The ocean was a crystal clear blue that was enticing and the white-washed architecture was quaint and distinctly Greek.

By the time the cab stopped in front of a cute little cottage, Ben had a smile on his face, fully looking forward to his time here.

The island had already charmed him.

He got out tipped the driver handsomely for the ride and put the key in the little blue door to what was to be his home for the next two weeks.

Inside, he saw it was tiny, with one main living-cum-kitchen area and a couple of doors on either side of that.

And then, much to Ben's surprise, out of one walked a pretty woman in a white bikini and an open red silk robe.

CHAPTER SEVEN

*W*hat the hell....?

The strange woman gave a startled cry and dropped her coffee, and Ben dropped his luggage as she jumped back.

She wrapped the robe tightly around herself and rushed over behind the counter in the kitchen.

"Who are you? What are you doing here?" she cried.

"I could you ask the same. I am staying here for the next two weeks," he pointed out.

"*I* have this place for the next two weeks!" she declared, eyeing him dangerously, and he noticed she had moved quite close to the knife block.

Ben could understand that, as any woman finding a strange man in her lodgings would want some sort of defence. But still...

He raised his hands in deference. "Hey, I will double-check the information I was given, but I suggest we both call our people and figure out what the hell is going on, okay?" he suggested.

His earlier frustration was back and he wasn't even hungry, he thought as he found Kimberly's number.

The woman facing him was digging through her purse keeping an eye on him as she pulled out her own phone.

While the call went through he went out the front door.

"Ben, do you have any idea what time it is here?" Kimberly grumbled. "Shouldn't you be on the beach or something?"

She sounded like he had woken her up. Good, he nodded to himself.

"I just thought I should fill you in on how my trip is going, Kim. The flight was wonderful; First Class was a nice touch by the way. The airline did lose my bags but they found them again, and just now I walked into your place and scared the hell out of a woman who is already staying here - supposedly also for the next two weeks. What do you think so far?" His frustration and sarcasm were on full blast.

"Jesus Ben, are you kidding me? I don't believe this. I made the reservation myself. Okay, hold tight and I will make some calls to the management company and get back to you. We will be able to figure things out," she told him.

His news had immediately transformed his agent from asleep to alert and on the ball. That made him feel a little better.

"All right. Just hurry, please. The woman jumped and almost dumped her coffee all over me. She is not happy," Ben told her.

"I will do my best and if I have to I will get cranky with someone," Kimberly finished before hanging up.

Ben paced outside to give the other tenant a chance to make her calls before heading back in. He felt strange just loitering outside the front door like that.

"Okay Carole, just make sure they call me soon, will you?" he heard her say from the other room.

Then she came out to him, shutting her phone down. She had changed into a long flowing red and blue patterned skirt and white T-shirt. He had to admit she was very attractive - under that silk robe especially.

Ben held up his phone. "I am waiting for my agent to call me back. She offered me this place; said it's a family timeshare," he explained.

"My aunt booked me, she is part of the share too," she told him in return. They stood there for a moment in awkward silence.

"There's some coffee just made if you want some," the woman offered hesitantly.

"That would be great." Ben smiled gratefully and went back inside the cottage to pour a cup. "I've been travelling for hours and it already feels like it's been a very long day."

She glanced at his luggage. "You've just come from the airport?"

"Yes, and it was one helluva trip."

After taking a long drink of coffee, Ben sighed in satisfaction. "Thank you. That tastes wonderful. I really am sorry about this. Hopefully, we can get things worked out quickly," he said, and she nodded.

"Me too. Aunt Carole claims the calendar was free, that was why she booked it," she said by way of explanation.

"I think that is why my agent reserved it for me," he said.

"Your travel agent?"

"No my literary agent. My name is Ben Norton, I am a writer. I came here to try and find something ..." he told her cryptically, pointing to his head.

She grinned shyly. "I'm Olivia Clarke, an accountant and I am trying to lose something," she said pointing to her own head.

They both got a chuckle out of that, which immediately broke the ice.

"So, have you seen the view?" Olivia asked going to the sliding glass doors. Ben had not noticed, but now that he could see the ocean he followed her out.

The coastal view across the caldera and out to the volcano was truly spectacular, and a little way down he could see direct access to a walkway along the beach.

Damn, he thought, this was nice. Kimberly had pulled out all the stops.

"I am positive I have never had a view quite like this," he admitted.

"I know. If it comes down to it, I may well arm wrestle you for it," the woman called Olivia said, although Ben was not certain if she was joking or not.

They stood in silence after that, sipping coffee and enjoying the warm breeze and the magnificent view. Then a phone rang.

Ben looked at his iPhone and knew it wasn't his. She did the same and then looked at him in surprise. The ringing continued and they quickly realised it was coming from inside.

He followed Olivia and saw a phone on the end table. A landline. She looked at him and he shrugged, so she picked it up.

"Hello, this is Olivia Clarke," he heard her say.

After a beat, she glanced at him. "Okay, thank you …

yes he is here too. All right, just a moment," she said and put her hand over the receiver.

"It is Greek TimeShare Management from Athens. They want me to put this on speaker so they can talk to both of us," she told him.

Ben shrugged. "Sure, let's see what they have to say," he told her.

He had a feeling it wasn't good though. Otherwise, Kimberly would be calling to brag about what a great job she had done securing the place for him alone and getting Olivia kicked out.

"Hello Mr. Norton, as I was just telling Miss Clarke, there has been a terrible mix-up. It seems the cottage was indeed booked by both Kimberly McNaughton and Carole Clarke. Somehow the system did not record either one, and as of a moment ago, the calendar is still showing the house as still available. We here at TimeShare Management are truly sorry for the confusion and would like to make it up to you. Our people have made many calls to try to find another available lodging in Santorini for either of you, but I'm afraid we have run into a snag ..." the man added hesitantly.

"Go on," Olivia told him, looking dubious.

"Well it's summer in Santorini - the middle of the tourist season and there is not a vacant bed available on all of the island. We were wondering ... if we managed to arrange some complimentary facilities - such as meals in some of our partner restaurants and entertainment for you both - if you would mind perhaps, sharing the bungalow for the ten-day crossover period of your stay?" he outlined with trepidation.

Ben looked at Olivia and she back at him. She had a calculating look in her eyes and he wondered if he would soon be arm-wrestling with her over it.

He sighed.

Yep. Helluva first day.

CHAPTER EIGHT

*M*uch later that evening, Ben woke in the smallest bedroom in the bungalow.

As it seemed their individual reservations coincided by about ten days, and with no other accommodation available on the island, he and Olivia had little choice but to tell the management company they would try sharing the place for a day or two to see how things went.

The translation of that, he thought was, 'see if they were in each other's way'.

Olivia had told him she would be out and about most days in any case, which was good for him.

Ben liked to work from early morning to mid-afternoon, sometimes later. This first day was a waste as far as work was concerned however, because between his lost luggage, jet lag as well as the problems with the bungalow, all he'd wanted to do was sleep.

He checked his phone and saw it was now about six pm Greek time.

Just in time for dinner, he thought, pleased. He got up and went into the main living area. He called out, but it appeared that his new roommate was as good as her word and was indeed out and about.

Ben grabbed some clean clothes and went into the single bathroom alongside the other bedroom - Olivia's 'side'.

He took a quick shower, enjoying the feeling of getting clean after the long trip. He finished shaving at the sink and got dressed before leaving the bathroom and was glad he had.

Olivia was sitting on the couch reading a magazine. She looked up at him, her face looking a little impatient.

"Hi. I just came back to change for dinner. Enjoy the shower?" she asked, immediately standing up and picking up a change of clothes on the couch next to her.

She had obviously been waiting for him to finish and was now *very* obviously annoyed by his hogging the bathroom.

Ben restrained from releasing a heavy sigh: clearly, they would have to work on their timing.

"Great water pressure," he answered lightly. "It felt amazing after the day I've had so far. Can you recommend a good place to eat around here?" he added conversationally.

Olivia nodded, moving towards the bathroom.

"Hali's is my favourite. It's just down the beach to the right when you get to the bottom of the trail off the veranda. It's about a half-mile walk down the steps to the coastline, and there is a whole string of cafés and tavernas along the beach," she informed him. "I tried out the management company's promise to compensate us at the partner restaurants they mentioned, and at the one I went to earlier they were falling all over themselves. So I don't think it will be a problem." She chuckled, looking a little more relaxed. "Hali's is on the list too. As far as I can tell almost every taverna down there is - have fun," she finished and headed into the bathroom.

Ben went into his room and put away his old clothes, then grabbed his wallet and phone before heading out to the veranda.

As the first time, stepping up to the railing was breathtaking.

The crystal clear water below against the darker colour of the volcanic rock was spectacular. He saw a few white sails silhouetted against the volcano in the distance and wondered what it would be like to spend a day on the water.

He then headed out the side gate off the veranda and down the path as Olivia described.

Just below, the path became steps and he followed about a hundred of them down to the walkway by the shore and out onto the beach.

As he walked along the coastline everything seemed like a treat for his senses. The water lapping up onto the shore. The feel of soft sand underfoot as he walked.

The scent of the evening sea air was invigorating, and despite the shaky start to the trip, now he felt an automatic bounce in his step.

He waved a greeting to a couple walking the other way, holding hands and taking turns throwing a frisbee for a little dog. They waved back with big smiles and he found himself smiling too.

His troubles did not feel so troubling walking down this beautiful Greek beach.

As he came up to the line of eateries he spied Hali's, the place Olivia had mentioned. It was a pretty whitewashed taverna with blue and white striped awnings fringed with bright pink bougainvillea, and open on the beach side with some tables beneath the awning or further inside.

Ben grabbed the only free outside table left so he could

see the beach and passersby. The place was filling up fast and he was glad for Olivia's suggestion.

The restaurant felt comfortable and easygoing, yet he was excited at the same time. He rarely left the States and when he had in the past it had been for book tours with no chance at all for any sightseeing or downtime.

Maybe exploring Santorini a little, and perhaps even some boating would spark his creativity and be good for his imagination? he thought, as he ordered some red wine and looked over the menu.

"I wanted to ask first …" he said to the Greek waiter who took the order. "I am staying at the bungalow further up the hill. There was a mix-up with my reservation and the management company said …" The man grinned and immediately nodded in agreement.

"Ah yes of course. We were told. It is terrible about your lodgings. But at least you have a lovely roommate and all you can eat, yes?" he joked.

"You know Olivia?" Ben asked, surprised.

"Yes, she has been here a few times over the last couple of days. She was here for coffee earlier and we discussed the issue. She has fallen in love with our Sfakianopita. You may wish to try it for dessert sir, after your dinner of course," the man added, then seemed to realise he might be talking too much.

But Ben did not mind. As a writer, he was an observer, but also a converser. "I was pretty annoyed when I found they had double booked the cottage, but it definitely could be worse. Olivia is pleasant enough," he admitted to the man and looked back down at the menu.

"Do you mind if I take a minute to choose?" he asked. There was so much on the menu that looked good he could not decide.

"Of course not. Please, take your time and I will return shortly," said the waiter with a slight bow.

It took a few minutes and a full glass of wine for Ben to make his decision. He finally decided on Giouvetsi: a lamb dish baked in a clay pot that came with fresh vegetables and bread. The waiter duly took his order and said he was wise for such an excellent choice.

Ben was sure the Greek man told everyone the same thing but ordered another glass of wine regardless.

Watching the many people wandering along the path by the beach, he suddenly spied Olivia and could not help but wave. She had recommended this place to him after all.

Spotting him, she made her way over to his table.

"Hello there. I see you found it. Sorry about waiting outside the bathroom like that. I realised later that it must have seemed very rude," she apologised. "I should have just waited in my room and not come across as so impatient."

Ben had already forgotten all about the incident and shook his head.

"No problem. If anything I should be apologising to you for hogging the bathroom. And I should thank you for your recommendation. I am enjoying Hali's tremendously so far. Enjoyed your day?" he added, smiling.

"Yes, I swam in the sea a lot earlier and it always feels good to get cleaned up."

Ben's waiter reappeared at the table. "Ah Olivia, how good to see you again. Are you joining your friend this evening?" he asked and she looked startled and a little flustered.

"I was just saying hello, Ramone," she told the waiter but Ben had noticed the traffic on the beach, and how quickly the restaurants had filled up in advance of the sunset.

She would be lucky to find anywhere at this point.

"You are more than welcome to join me if you want. It is looking like finding a table here or elsewhere may be a bit of a wait. Not to mention you would have gotten out sooner if I hadn't held you up earlier," he added with a wink.

He was surprised by his own forthrightness but went with his instincts.

As soon as he said it, Ben realised he would actually like some company.

Someone to compare notes with about the locals and tourists would be enjoyable on this balmy summer Greek evening.

CHAPTER NINE

*O*livia looked hesitant, glancing down the beach and around the crowded restaurant.

"The place does look busy tonight. Are you sure you don't mind, Ben? We did promise to stay out of each other's way ..."

He could see she was just trying to be courteous too and he reflected that there was nothing worse than two people trying to be nice to each other in situations like this - people trying to be kind but ending up cancelling out each other's efforts.

He put a hand over his heart.

"I swear - on my next book - I really would enjoy the company," he promised with sincerity in his tone.

She seemed to believe him and relaxed, nodding. Ben

immediately got up and pulled out her chair and from behind her, Ramone the waiter winked at him.

Olivia ordered a glass of red wine and already seemed to know what she wanted. She asked the waiter for something called a Kokkininsto and Ben recalled from the menu that it was a sort of stew.

Ramone quickly came back with her glass of wine and she thanked him. Typically courteous, he bowed to her before moving on to his other customers.

"It did not seem as busy before, but of course, it is the weekend now. Thank you for the offer Ben, at least I know the food is always good here," she said and paused then laughed. "Listen to me, I act like I have been in Santorini forever instead of just a couple of days." She giggled a little, then took a sip of wine.

Despite the setback with the accommodation she was obviously enjoying her stay immensely. The mix-up with the cottage aside, Ben had already started to think he was going to enjoy this place too.

Particularly if he could get cracking on a decent story.

"You have been here longer than I have, so you are a veteran compared to me. May I ask what you have seen so far?" he asked curious as to what sort of adventures she had gotten up to since her arrival.

It turned out that in the three days previous Olivia had already explored a lot of the little town they were in, more so than he would want to in so little time, Ben thought.

She was completely taken with the place though.

Their food came at the same time and they each ordered another glass of wine and dug in. For Ben, the food was even better than it had been on his arrival in Greece in the early hours of that morning. He and Olivia relished their food with equal satisfaction as he finished his description of his travel adventures before reaching the island.

"I suppose the bright side is they still had your luggage," Olivia chuckled. "Could you imagine if your bags were on their way to Nome, Alaska or somewhere equally unreachable?"

He had to admit she was right. Things could have gone a lot worse.

"You have a point. And I have been to Nome actually. It was beautiful, but a bit out of reach of most things, though the inhabitants seem to like it that way. I would probably never get my luggage back though, and some Alaskan would get to live out his days in my beloved Gucci loafers" he joked.

After the main course, they both ordered the Sfakianopita - on Olivia's recommendation - and a coffee. It was the perfect finish to a delicious meal. The honey in the desert complimented the coffee nicely.

"Wonderful Olivia - great choice. You are turning out to be a fantastic tour guide," Ben told her and she laughed.

It was a sweet sound, particularly in this setting, he thought.

"Well, thank you. Though I'm afraid I have told you everything I know about the island so far. I will repeat however the naps in hammocks on the beach are fast becoming a daily thing. Lazy cocktails too... heaven," she added with gusto.

He laughed with her and thought he may well have to try that too.

He hadn't been kidding when he'd said she'd make a great tour guide. He was enjoying talking to her and would quite happily sit there for another glass or two except for the yawn that suddenly came out of him.

"Sorry, I couldn't help it. I think I am going to head back," he told her apologetically.

"Thanks for letting me share your table," Olivia said as he stood up. "I think I am going to stay on here for a bit. But I will be leaving the cottage in the morning early for a yoga class and then breakfast and I may not be back until later in the day so you will have the place to yourself," she added reassuringly.

"No worries, and somehow I think our roommate thing will work out just fine. Enjoy your evening and I will see you sometime tomorrow."

. . .

BEN STROLLED LEISURELY BACK along the beach enjoying the cooler breeze and the sounds of laughter and fun from the people he passed.

He saw the same couple with the frisbee from before and waved to them again and they returned it with grins. He was hard-pressed to remember ever meeting such happy-go-lucky friendly folks.

Everyone here seemed so cheery and cordial. It was a pleasant change from the hustle and bustle of NYC.

When Ben got back to the bungalow he looked in the refrigerator and saw glass bottles of water, frosty cold.

He grabbed one and went into his bedroom, then sat on the bed to read for a bit and let his brain switch off a little before sleep. It was an engrossing read about an exploration of the Ozark Mountains. The tale had seemed farfetched when it was referred to him, but now he was entirely caught up in it.

He hardly heard when Olivia came back a little while later. Merely the rustling of her steps and the sound of the veranda doors alerted him to her presence.

Soon it was pitch dark and he was reading by the light of the bedside lamp. He did not turn off the light until almost midnight and felt it had been a long but satisfying day, despite everything.

Or maybe because of everything?

As he felt himself drift off, he wondered what a man going out on the waters around these parts in a fishing boat would find.

What sort of mysteries could be discovered?

Ben did not know it, but he went to sleep with a peaceful smile on his face.

CHAPTER TEN

The following morning, Olivia thanked the yoga instructor when her class finished.

For the last few days, doing yoga as the sun was coming up over the cliffs and bathing the island in its soft morning glow had been relaxing and exhilarating at the same time.

She said goodbye to her classmates and strolled off down the beach. This time she went in the other direction to find breakfast and explore a little more.

She was enjoying all the walking since arriving here, and keeping herself so occupied had helped her move away from moping over her ex.

About a half mile down the beach and up a side road of cobblestones further into the village, she found a café that looked good called Herodias Harmonies. She had an egg meal with potatoes and some of the wonderful toasted Greek bread.

Afterwards, she sipped coffee and watched the people strolling the whitewashed bougainvillea-lined streets in the morning sunshine.

She had gone back to the bungalow about an hour after Ben last night and had been surprised to find he was still up. His door was open and he was reading and had not seemed to notice her moving through the living room.

So she got some iced tea and sat on the veranda, watching the stars over the caldera and just enjoying the nighttime air.

He was an interesting guy, she thought now, sipping her coffee. He was very polite and quite reasonable considering the predicament they had found themselves in.

They seemed to get along OK so far, and she agreed with him in that she did not think there would be any problem with them sharing the cottage for the duration of their respective trips.

Granted, at first the idea of having a strange man in the house had horrified her and made her immediately worried for her safety, but yet there was something about the confident and no-nonsense way Ben had handled things that was reassuring.

And once she found out he was a famous writer - and a

celebrity of sorts - she suspected he would hardly do anything to risk his reputation.

She wasn't sure why, but her instincts told her to trust him.

Perhaps because he was so very different from Derek?

Both men were handsome but had completely different personalities. Derek was very forceful and commanding and completely believed in his own right-eousness.

That was why Olivia had come to believe it had never occurred to him that sleeping with her best friend was something he shouldn't do.

He had never considered that there was anything he couldn't do if he wanted to.

Ben seemed so much more easy-going and open to enjoyment for the pure fun of it. There did not have to be a purpose behind it.

She wondered if that was his artist self showing. She imagined that being a writer would necessitate the ability to be open-minded.

Olivia realised then that she was indulging in whimsy; it was not like she knew Ben well or anything.

She just did not see any resemblance to Derek in him, and that was a good thing. Not only did she not need the reminder as a roommate, Derek really was a dick and she didn't need that either.

She was beginning to think like Carole, and wondering what the hell had she been doing with the guy in the first place. Olivia's heart gave a little tremble then, reminding her that she had loved Derek after all.

That was what she had been doing with him.

There had been a time when Derek had been nice, complimentary and even generous. She wondered now if all of that had been for show. Bait for the prize he wanted maybe. In any case, she would never know, or did she need to know?

Sod it, she decided. That was enough heavy thinking for today.

She had beaches to stroll and hammocks to nap in. Olivia felt herself smile at the thought and she got up to pay and continue on with another day in paradise.

DESPITE THE NUMEROUS signs and kiosks advertising same, she'd decided against parasailing or boat trips around the volcano.

At least for the moment.

She was hoping to get up the gumption to maybe try something more adventurous at some point though.

As she strolled down the beach she took off the linen cover-up she had on so she was only wearing her shorts and her bikini top. It was a bargain she had made to herself. Get used to one half of the bikini and then maybe she could risk the other half.

From the looks she was getting from the male locals and tourists as she walked along though, she had a feeling no one had a problem with it.

She also knew her reticence was a hangover of sorts from Derek. He had preferred that she keep mostly covered up and she now believed that far from modesty concerns, it was more of a possessive thing.

He thought she was his and no one could see her the way he got to.

Idiot, she snorted to herself as she reached the hammock stations. After four days in a row, the owner of the stand smiled when he saw her coming.

"I have been telling people, I have found the perfect customer. Miss Olivia - *she* understands what I have to offer. They do not believe I could find such a great customer!" Little Iason was a black-haired, stocky Greek with a permanent smile on his face and a cheerful nature that was infectious.

"Don't you think you are going overboard just a bit, Iason?" she asked laughing.

"No, not at all Miss Olivia. You understand the need for the peace and solitude my hammocks provide. It is an inspiration to me that I have chosen the right profession. Would you like your usual hammock and cocktail?" he asked solicitously.

"Of course. I'll want to live up to your kind words," she told him.

She took her icy drink to her preferred hammock frontline to the beach and got comfortable.

Taking a sip of her pina colada she smiled. She had always been a creature of habit and being here in Santorini had not changed that.

Derek used to complain she was boring and predictable and it had bothered her. She was beginning to think he was wrong on that front as well.

Just because she did like some structure, it did not mean everything she did was predictable and hell, even if it was, it was her life.

Olivia took another drink of the creamy refreshing pineapple drink, set it on the table and lay back, watching the water lap softly onto the shore.

All too soon she floated away into a dream of splashing water on a white-sailed boat in the Santorini waters, laughing.

CHAPTER ELEVEN

hen she awoke she was refreshed and ready for the rest of her day.

After a light Dakos salad for lunch, she strolled further down the beach and scoped out a cave that was once investigated by Jacques Cousteau, the great underwater explorer.

Apparently, he had gone looking for traces of the lost city of Atlantis. Santorini was situated on what was possibly the only live volcano to host a city and he thought the history of ancient eruptions could have been a clue to the lost city.

He had found nothing conclusive, and the last eruption on the island had been over three thousand years ago. The cave was magnificent though; all lava rock that led to an underground lake.

When she got back to the bungalow it was almost four o'clock and she found Ben sitting on the veranda with a beer, smiling and looking relaxed.

She returned the smile as he got up and opened the gate for her before she got there.

Unlike Derek, he was attentive and thoughtful too, she realised.

"Hi, I hope your writing day went well," she said as she came up onto the veranda, a little sweaty and out of breath.

Embarrassed, she only then realised she was carrying her blouse and was still in her bikini top.

Ben did not, like many men, let his eyes immediately stray to her chest and Olivia appreciated that. She was also aware that her hair was mussed and had come out of her ponytail and hung around her face, but he did not seem in the least bit affected by her unkempt appearance.

He seemed so easygoing and nice to be around that she had a feeling that rather than a thorn in her side, her new roommate might become a welcome companion.

"It was fantastic actually. Last night I had this brilliant idea for a story and just went wild with it. I may have to experience some more of this wonderful place to keep the creative juices flowing. How were your adventures today?" he asked her politely, offering her a beer.

Olivia accepted and took a drink, letting the icy liquid cool her a little.

"Great, did some sunrise yoga, had some great food as well as a little sightseeing - and most importantly, my hammock nap and cocktail," she added with a smile.

He laughed. "Sounds idyllic. Well, the bathroom is all yours if you want it. I am done writing for the day and am gonna hunt down some food in a while. Have you tried the Café Eluent - about a mile down the beach? It's on the list and looks good. But more importantly, is the food any good?" he asked her taking another sip of beer.

"I haven't tried it but I saw it the other day. If you are still around later, I might pop in and join you for a drink?" she found herself saying.

He cracked open another bottle of beer. "Better yet, why don't I wait for you? I am in no hurry, this view can keep me occupied for some time," he said gesturing out at the Aegean Sea. "That's if you don't mind company again this evening."

"Actually I'd love that. Being on my own all day is nice, but can get quite quite boring."

"Ditto." He took another sip of beer and raised it in a toast to her.

"I won't be long," she said and Ben turned back to the sea as she went inside.

Olivia showered quickly and realised how easy it had

been for her to agree to go with him to dinner. She guessed they were at the beginning of a companionable friendship and she was surprised at how simple, yet pleasant an idea it was.

Then again, she thought as she lathered up, they were both tourists and in the same situation of having no choice but to share accommodation.

It gave them a commonality that would make getting along a more natural thing. Kind of an us against them sort of thing.

Oh well, either way, it's nice to have someone to talk to at dinner, she told herself as she rinsed out her hair and tried to decide what to wear for dinner with a handsome American she barely knew.

CHAPTER TWELVE

Olivia picked out a red summer dress, and flowing skirt with a thin waist sash and dried her hair, letting it down for a change.

Just a touch of makeup, she never liked piling it on, and she was ready to go.

When she came out Ben was waiting on the veranda but had also since changed into blue cotton pants and a white, short-sleeved, linen shirt. She gulped a little at the sight of him. He was very handsome.

They walked down the beach together smiling and waving at various locals and other tourists that Olivia had gotten used to seeing. Ben pointed out one couple with a dog, holding hands and smiling.

"I saw them here yesterday too," he commented as they exchanged waves.

"They've been around since I got here. I think they are locals just revelling in the fact they live in such an amazing place," she said looking at him.

"I think you're right and it reminds me we should all appreciate where we come from. I am from New York City and few cities can compare to it, yet I hardly think that way. You are from London, right?" he asked.

She nodded, realising they had never actually talked about where they were from."Oy, how can ya tell guv'na?" she joked in her best Cockney accent.

Ben laughed.

"Just a guess. You do have a lovely accent though. I visited London on a book tour once and always wished I had taken the time to look around. It is a pretty spectacular place too," he complimented.

"It is and you are right. It is easy to forget the things we have and always look for something else. Humans are weird," she said.

"True enough and thank goodness for that - it gives me plenty of material to write about," he quipped and she laughed.

When they got to the taverna Ben mentioned, it was one of the few enclosed restaurants on the seafront, but they were early enough to get a good window seat facing the beach. That and the management company had pulled out all the stops because here too, they got the red carpet treatment.

Olivia had to admit this was a nice touch by the company and was going a long way to making up for the problem with the cottage.

She and Ben ordered a nice wine and then went with the house special of broiled fish and herbs, with a rice and veggie dish.

As they settled into their wine, a man approached their table. His hesitant tone and the fact that he was carrying a book, suggested to Olivia that he was possibly a fan of Ben's.

Hi, you're Ben Norton, yes?" The thin man asked hesitantly in a Scottish accent.

Ben smiled and looked up at him. "That is what my mom named me," he responded cheerfully.

"I am such a huge fan. I was wondering if you could sign my copy of *Surrogate Damage*. I love how you wind it up at the end. I can't believe I was sitting over there re-reading it then looked up and the same guy on the cover was actually sitting in this restaurant," he said excitedly. "I'm such a fan."

Ben reached out and took the book and the pen from him. He opened the cover while Olivia just watched quietly, sipping her wine. The thin man did not appear to have noticed her and she thought that was funny.

"What is your name, I could put "to fan" but that would be weird even for me," Ben joked.

The man laughed nervously. "Oh yeah, sorry. I'm Jack and I am from Glasgow, Scotland," he said.

"Good to meet you Jack from Glasgow. I hope you are enjoying Santorini," Ben said as he wrote something in the book before signing it with a flourish.

"I am; it is my first holiday in Greece. There is so much to do and see, I feel like I don't want to leave," Jack said.

"I know what you mean. It is a beautiful place. Here you go. I hope your vacation continues to be great for you," he told him.

"Thanks, mate, I appreciate you taking the time. I see the new book is coming out at Christmas - I am looking forward to that," Jack added with an eager look in his eyes.

Olivia was taken aback. From what little Ben had said he had only just started writing it. She glanced at him but he showed no sign of nervousness or hesitation.

"That is the plan. I hope you like it as much as you did *Surrogate*. Have a great evening," he said with a smile.

Jack left then and Ben shrugged.

"Sorry about that. I don't usually get recognised by readers, but when I do they can be … determined," he said as dinner was brought over.

"No worries. I found it an interesting experience to behold, to be honest. I have never been near a real-life celebrity. I need to read one of your books to keep up," she laughed.

Ben smiled, not at all put out that she had not known who he was. She had a vague memory of hearing his name upon meeting him yesterday, but that was it.

They started in on the fish and it too was excellent. Though being inside the restaurant was stifling and she missed the breeze off the water.

"I thought you handled his last question well. Didn't you just start writing your new book?" she asked.

He nodded and looked a little disgruntled. "Yep. Just today actually. I would have appreciated my publisher letting me know they'd set a release date. Probably figured I wouldn't hear about it in Greece," he said. There was annoyance in his eyes for a brief moment, but it was quickly followed by amusement.

"It is that whole Stephen King thing," he told her, as she swallowed her bite of fish.

"Stephen King thing?" Olivia asked. She'd heard of that writer of course.

Ben nodded and dipped his bread in the sauce.

"Yeah, King went and said in his book, *On Writing* - an excellent book by the way, kind of his life story - that writing a book should take no longer than three months. But people - editors in particular - tend to overlook the fact he was discussing how *he* writes. Most of us have different time frames. Anyway, something like that enabled publishers to whine if you don't get it done in quick time," he said with another shrug and took a bite of his sauce-soaked bread.

"It does seem wrong for people to use such a prolific writer as a benchmark. Let's face it, even I know he's written practically hundreds of books at this stage," Olivia said in agreement. She then dipped her bread in the sauce and they were both silent as they finished up their meal.

Afterwards, they both leaned back in contentment.

"If it is okay, I was going to ask what your new book is about, but I am not sure about the protocol surrounding such questions," she said. She knew she never would have asked such a thing before, but Ben was such good company and the wine was so good she figured, why not?

He chuckled. "I don't mind at all. I just have a rough plot outlined, but basically, I'm fascinated by those white sailboats you see out on the water all the time. So far my story is about a man who takes a boat and goes out searching for something," he told her, and she noticed his voice softened a little as he said it.

Olivia realised with a start that he was really trusting her by telling her that much and she resolved to not abuse that trust. She of all people knew how that felt.

"Searching for what?" she asked and he shrugged.

"I have no idea. I want to be just as surprised writing it as hopefully readers will be reading it."

"That makes sense. But you could always rent a boat yourself and see what's out there in reality. I took a cave tour today and there's been stories around here about the Lost City of Atlantis."

He laughed surprised. "Here? I'll be damned. I will admit I had been thinking of taking one out though. I do know how to sail - I used to take a boat up and down the Hudson River so maybe they would let me have one for a bit," he said thoughtfully. "So would you be interested in a trip out on the Aegean, Olivia?" he asked then.

She was surprised, but he was so casual about it that she felt herself nodding before she'd even thought about it properly.

"That would be fun, I think. Thanks for the invitation, when would you like to go?"

"I was thinking maybe once I've got some more words under my belt. How does the middle of next week sound? Though I don't want to take away from your plans…" he added then, a little more hesitant.

"Sure. The only thing I've got planned while here is sunrise yoga every morning and my hammock in the afternoon along with a few tourist trips here and there. Other than that, I would be only too happy to accompany you," she told him.

Their eyes met then and Olivia felt a frisson from Ben's appreciative glance, as well as a warmth from his respect and consideration, which she was not used to.

In hindsight, Derek the Dick had not been big on appreciation or respect.

CHAPTER THIRTEEN

The following Thursday morning, Olivia finished her last fifteen minutes of yoga, stretching and watching the boats in the lagoon Ben had mentioned.

She took deep breaths as they sailed by, or in the case of one colossal one, just stop and stare. It was a beautiful yacht, huge with a small skiff on the back.

As her last deep breathing exercises finished, the skiff was lowered and began making its way to the beach with people on board.

She said goodbye to her classmates and looked around for Ben who had said he would meet her after her class.

Today they were taking the boat trip he'd suggested, and she was looking forward to it more than she'd anticipated.

For the last week or so they'd pretty much kept themselves to themselves while Ben worked hard on his book, and Olivia worked hard on her tan.

They'd met up for the occasional coffee or drink on the veranda, but Ben was throwing himself into his writing and had no choice but to temporarily eschew Santorini's many attractions in favour of hard work.

Strangely, Olivia found she was missing his company and the cheerful camaraderie they'd shared in the early days of his arrival.

She was also more than a little bereft that her escape to this magnificent island would be coming to an end in little under a week.

The first ten days had flown by.

She drank some water as she looked down the beach for Ben. Then she heard his voice and turning, she saw him walk across the sand looking handsome in khaki board shorts and a white T-shirt.

"I hope I am not late. Did you have a good session?" he asked pleasantly.

"I did. It was blissful, and very relaxing. I decided I'm going to start a yoga routine when I get back to London. How has your week gone?" she asked as they walked down the beach a little way.

"Great actually - would you believe I got twenty-five-thousand words out? And I found the perfect boat, but they won't let me sail it." He frowned. "The open water is a little different from the Hudson River, though the Greeks obviously have never tried it," he added wryly. "So I got us a personal tour instead. Meals and a captain to show us around. Are you still game?"

Olivia nodded, encouraged by the idea until Ben pointed to a tiny little vessel on the shore about twenty-five yards away. She hesitated a little, seeing a man standing next to it in the clear waves.

"Meals too?" she repeated eyebrows raising, and he looked at the boat and then back at her before he got it.

Then he laughed out loud.

"No, no that is our taxi - to that," he said and pointed out to the big cruiser yacht she had been admiring earlier.

Immediately, Olivia felt herself blushing. "Oh crikey, sorry about that. You said a personal tour boat and pointed to the guy and the dinghy ..." she tried to explain, and Ben just shook his head chuckling.

"You should have seen the look on your face." He put his arm out to her and she took it. "Come, my friend. Let us check out the high seas," he added and they went and climbed into the little dinghy. "Breakfast is waiting,"

CHAPTER FOURTEEN

The sailor smiled and greeted her in Greek and Olivia realised he did not speak any English.

She managed a good morning in Greek but that was as good as it got as to her shame, she had not spent enough time learning the language.

The Greek man rowed them out to the big cruiser where a small platform and then short steps led them up to the main deck.

The captain who much to her relief introduced himself in perfect English as Captain Kastor, welcomed them on board. He then took Olivia on a tour while Ben trailed along, presumably having already seen it all before renting it.

Olivia was amazed at the luxuriousness of the vessel. The yacht had four guest cabins, several bathrooms, a fishing and sun deck, as well as a dining room and lounge. It was a small floating palace and she loved it.

She had seen pictures of boats like this in magazines but had never thought she would be on one.

She felt a bit like a celebrity - especially on the arm of a famous bestselling author! Wait until she told Aunt Carole...

When the captain left them on the lounge deck to get going, she turned to Ben.

"The management company paid for this?" she queried. The company had also offered them some tour options, but even for them this seemed a bit much.

Ben laughed. "I don't think it was included in the entertainment budget. Don't worry, I owe you not only for your remarkable patience and kindness in letting me share the cottage but also for your friendship. And I would have rented it anyway so you may as well come along. Don't worry about the cost," he said.

"What do you mean you owe me? I didn't do anything," she told him as the boat began moving through the water and heading out towards the open water, away from the coastline.

"You have been so positive and adventurous in your approach to this place that it inspired me to do the same, and now I am getting ideas left and right. So thank you. Like I said, I would have come out anyway so I am glad for the company," he told her, his dark eyes burning into hers.

Olivia blushed slightly but then the wind picked up and blew her ponytail around her face, breaking the moment. She laughed, gathered it back and tied it up better, then she pulled a wide-brimmed hat out of her big bag and put that on.

It almost blew off and she held it on with her hand.

"I think you may be fighting a losing battle there. Hungry?" Ben asked and she remembered the food.

They went back inside into a dining area where a tremendous spread had been laid out for them. Fruit, pieces of bread, juices and champagne. They were able to watch their progress out the wide windows while they ate.

"He's going to take us to what is supposed to be a good fishing spot. Do you mind?" Ben asked her.

Olivia finished the bagel she was eating and shook her head. "Not at all. It is your charter. And your research. Besides, I have never been sea fishing before. Should be fun," she replied with a grin.

The fishing deck was on the lower section of the boat and had rod holders and fishing chairs all setup. Olivia was more taken with the wide expanse of blue water than the fishing, but like she had told Ben, she was willing to give it a go.

The two sat companionably in the fishing chairs with

the rods in holders which seemed a little bit like cheating. At least it did until Olivia realised deep sea poles were heavy and much longer than regular fishing rods. She would be lucky to hold one up for a few seconds, much less wrestle a fish with it. Unfortunately, they did not get a bite.

She and Ben hardly noticed though, pointing to distant isles or some of the bigger fish they could see in the water.

None of them went for the bait but at least they got to see some, she thought with amusement. Ben found it funny as well.

Occasionally another sailboat would pass by and everyone would wave excitedly to one another as if it was a huge deal to see someone out on the water.

"Why do you think that is?" Olivia asked. "I mean we don't know them, they don't know us and we are passing at a pretty good clip. That last boat was really moving, so why get so excited?"

Ben thought about it and chuckled.

"Good question. You always have an interesting way of coming at things. Let's see, maybe they are just showing off. The young guy holding the rudder looked like the type to want to brag, the women were having a good time and probably just waving for the hell of it. But it could also have come out of tradition originally, signalling passing boats for safety and respect. And modern man has transformed into a ritual of bragging," he finished.

She looked at him a long time, thinking about what he said, then raised her eyebrows in amusement.

"Did you just make that up off the top of your head - about the tradition?" she asked and he laughed.

"Well, yeah. It is what I do for a living you know," he joked, a twinkle in his eye.

When the captain came back down he said he did not know why people on passing boats got so excited. He did say older, more mature people, just waved politely, and did not jump up and down.

Olivia glanced amusedly at Ben who was listening closely.

He nudged her playfully. "I was right then. Young braggarts. You see Olivia, sometimes it pays to use your imagination," he teased, laughing at himself.

She smiled, enjoying herself immensely.

By lunch, they gave up on fishing and were more into sightseeing. By the end of the day, Olivia felt like she'd seen more of the islands than the Greeks themselves, and had done more laughing with Ben in a short few hours than she had over the last few months.

It truly was a perfect day.

CHAPTER FIFTEEN

$\mathcal{B}$y the time they got back to the cottage, the sun was not more than half an hour from setting.

Olivia had been under the hot rays all day, had a wonderful time and had seen many wonderful things that had kept her mind busy, but she felt well and truly shattered.

Ben looked at her as he put the key in the door.

"I am going to go put on some coffee if you want the first shower. I'm exhausted, but I don't want to crash this early or I will be up at three am," he said.

She smiled tiredly and nodded as they entered the living room. She was not going to argue. A cool shower sounded fantastic and she gathered her clothes and proceeded to the bathroom.

Once in the water, she sighed. The cool water felt like heaven and she stretched out her muscles as the water ran over her. If it had not been for sunscreen she would have been toast.

It had been a fantastically enjoyable and fun-filled day, she had to say.

She and Ben had visited two smaller islands close to Santorini and were able to take a look at an archaeological site. Nothing related to the Lost City of Atlantis, so Ben was a little disappointed about that.

She smiled. He was great company and was turning into a wonderful holiday companion.

When she felt refreshed and clean, she dried off and got dressed, putting on a long silk dress she'd bought especially for the holiday.

It was purple and white patterned, swirling around her body with a white and purple sash holding it in at her waist. She brushed out her hair and left it loose.

Tying it up on the boat had not helped, and her hair was in such a state so she might as well give up on it for the rest of the trip, she thought wryly.

"It is all yours, Ben," she said as she came out of the bathroom. Then she got a whiff of the coffee. "That smells heavenly."

He was sitting on the couch, writing by hand in a little book.

"It tastes even better if I do say so myself. How was the shower?" he asked without a break in his writing.

"Great. I left you some hot water, mostly because I didn't use much," she told him. He finished writing and closed his book.

"Boy am I looking forward to it. I will be out in a minute," he said standing and picking up a small stack of clothes he had ready.

He then went into the bathroom and she went for the coffee.

One sip and she was in heaven. The shower had been reinvigorating and the coffee was the perfect thing for the end of a busy day.

She went out on the veranda realising that it was not quite sundown yet. She leaned against the railing and just enjoyed the view. The waves were coming gently ashore, slow as if lazy from their busy day, and the fading light twinkled over the moving water making it appear almost solid, like a moving crystal sheet.

It was a lovely sight and she gasped, entranced.

She almost did not notice Ben joining her at the railing just as the sun was going down but felt her body instinctively flood with warmth as he appeared beside her.

"Good timing if I do say so myself," he said.

They both watched the sun lower into a red and

orange flame that seemed for an instant to spring up from the horizon, bidding them a good night.

Then it faded and Olivia sighed. She wasn't sure it got much better than that.

After a moment they both went and sat down, putting their feet up. Enjoying their coffee and the magnificent view.

"So how are the ideas coming after today?" she asked.

"Good. I wrote a section I have been going over in my head since this afternoon. I will type it up in the morning. My hero still doesn't know what he is looking for. Maybe he will never find it. You know, the journey is supposed to be the worthier goal," he said whimsically, and she laughed.

"I didn't know you were a poet too."

"Sometimes, depends on the stimulus. And there has been plenty of stimuli so far. Did you enjoy the trip, Olivia?" he asked glancing sideways at her.

"I did. I must admit I have never been in that much luxury before. That boat had everything. Pity no fish were biting," she said. She knew he had been hoping for that.

"No big deal. I don't think I will be going for a yacht that big next time. A nice sailboat would be better. You're closer to the water that way. I had a great time too though. Those islands were amazing and some of those caves are astounding," he added with enthusiasm.

Both of them were gradually waking up with the addition of coffee to their system.

"So," Ben continued after a beat, "you said when we first met that you were here to lose something. May I ask what?"

Olivia hesitated a moment. She hadn't mentioned that to anyone. Then again, Ben was confiding plot points in his upcoming book and had just spent the day wining and dining her in incredible luxury.

She owed him a little trust.

"Heartbreak over losing my fiancé," she admitted ashamedly.

"Ouch, sorry to hear that. Was it bad?" he asked both concerned and curious.

"Bad enough. He slept with my best friend two weeks before the wedding," she told him in a rush and then took a sip of her coffee.

Ben looked astounded at her words.

"Damn Olivia, I am so sorry. I have had bad relationships but...damn. Not much of a best friend huh?" He said it with just the right touch of support and humour so that his remark did not bother her.

She smiled slightly, grateful for this response. "You're telling me. Anyway, my aunt suggested this - coming here I mean. I think she'd already booked it for me before she called and offered," she said, realising this just at that very moment.

Aunt Carole had always had the knack of knowing just what Olivia needed before she knew it herself.

"Ah family, they do come in handy some days don't they?" Ben joked. He had taken her hint and pivoted away from her fiancé, and she realised he really was a true friend. A lot of people would have just kept prying.

"Yes, Aunt Carole is great. She has looked out for me ever since my folks died when I was sixteen. I had no idea what to expect when she offered. I've never been to a timeshare, much less in the Greek Islands."

She and Ben sipped their coffee for a little longer and then they both decided to call it a night.

Yet Olivia guessed that her confession had moved their relationship on from casual roommates to true friends.

She said goodnight and went into her room. It was stiflingly warm in there so she opened the window and for the first time since Ben's arrival, left her door open too.

She'd guessed from the outset that she didn't need to worry about him but now she knew for sure; Ben Norton was a true gentleman.

In the bathroom, she changed into a vest top and shorts and then climbed into bed, just lying there for a while before drifting off.

She enjoyed the faint sound of people still on the beach and of course the hypnotic sound of the waves lapping the shoreline.

Olivia fell asleep dreaming of a moonlit beach with sparkling waves and laughter while she walked hand in hand with a handsome stranger.

CHAPTER SIXTEEN

*B*en woke up in the early hours of the morning when it was still dark so he got up, made some coffee and began writing.

His mind was now well and truly bursting with his story and he had to get it down.

A couple of hours after he got up he could hear Olivia stirring in the other room. He registered it but kept going; they had talked the day before about meeting for breakfast after her yoga, so he had plenty of time, and just let the story come together on the screen.

When he felt he had enough written, he leaned back and sipped the remaining coffee in his cup. It was stone cold.

He got up, stretched and went out to the living room,

hardly able to believe he'd written so much in a single week. The book was almost halfway done already. Kim would be ecstatic.

Olivia had already left for the morning and looking at the clock, Ben realised he had stopped just in time.

He got cleaned up quickly and by the time he was ready to go, he was starving.

He trotted down the steps to the beach and returned a wave from the couple with the dog. The sun was bright and the water had that shimmering crystal sheen he enjoyed so much.

He could see sailboats out on the water and even saw the big yacht they had chartered the day before. He waved, knowing they probably could not see him. The wave was more for himself.

He approached Olivia's yoga class just as it was ending. His timing was good, he told himself. She saw him and smiled, then trotted down to the sand to meet him.

"Morning Ben. You were up early, get much done?" she asked, as they began walking side by side along the beach. He watched some kids splashing in the surf before looking down at her.

"I did, it was great actually. Something about this place is so invigorating when it comes to writing," he told her.

Of course, he told himself, this place wasn't the only

thing that invigorated him - he'd realised that for sure on the boat yesterday when he and Olivia had shared a moment just before she'd struggled to keep her hair under that hat.

Today she was wearing a patterned blouse tied at the waist and a matching skirt and sparkly sandals. Her hair was loose and blowing in the breeze, her eyes sparkled and she was the perfect picture of vibrancy.

Ben wanted to strangle the idiot fiancé who'd abandoned her and hurt her so.

Still, perhaps the guy's loss …

"So you mentioned a good breakfast place?" he asked conversationally.

"Yep, it is just up here. Any ideas what you want to do afterwards?" she replied.

"I do. I seem to recall you also mentioning a comfy hammock on the beach somewhere along here. After a whole night up writing, sounds like an experience I need. It has literally been years since I took a nap in the daytime," he laughed.

"Yes, after all the work you've done this week, I think you deserve it. And after yesterday I am looking forward to mine too. Especially after a big breakfast. This place is the best for those," she said and pointed up to the beach.

There was another open-air café just a few minutes

away. Beyond that, Ben saw a stand of palm trees and guessed that was where the hammocks must be.

He had never slept in a hammock either, but no doubt it would be an experience.

Everything involving Olivia tended to be.

CHAPTER SEVENTEEN

*H*ours later, Ben awoke from his slumber to the sounds of seagulls, lapping water, and the breeze through the leaves of the trees.

He stretched and yawned. It was an amazing way to get some sleep, he had to admit.

At first, he had thought there was no way he could sleep out in the open in public and in a hammock of all things.

Yet after the full breakfast Olivia mentioned, he had settled in and dozed off to the same sounds he awoke to.

He carefully got out of the hammock, having seen a tourist flip out of one when they had arrived. Olivia was already awake and sitting in hers.

She was fluffing out her hair and he realised how

much he enjoyed watching her do that. She was graceful in everything she did.

They spent the day wandering around the area - Ben enjoying his first well-earned day off in some time.

They took a bus across the island to a historical site similar to one they had seen from the water the day before, in which they found the crystalline stone and volcanic rock to be an interesting beautiful contrast.

They were shown a cave that was rumoured to have once been a haven for pirates which Ben found fascinating. Not to mention fun as he and Olivia joked in pirate for the rest of the afternoon, uttering "shiver me timbers" and "ay matey" with huge abandon and much laughter.

Later, they enjoyed another fantastic dinner at Hali's and after picking up a nice Greek wine, they both decided to head back to their veranda for the sunset.

They had enjoyed it so much from up there the night before they wanted to see it again.

So Ben found himself, feet up with a glass of wine watching a spectacular sunset next to a beautiful woman who had so effortlessly become his friend.

Not a bad way to end the day, he thought, taking a sip of his wine.

As the sun dropped lower the light did something different to the previous night. Instead of shooting up like a brief laser blast, this sunset spread itself out across the horizon in brilliant hues of red and orange and then slowly faded, leaving Ben and Olivia to admire the sparkling stars and reflection of the moon on the water.

"I never get tired of that," she said in awe.

"Me neither. It is amazing how we humans can forget things as simple yet majestic as the sunset," he said and held out his glass to her.

They clinked them together in a toast.

"To three more Santorini sunsets," Olivia said mournfully, obviously thinking of her imminent departure.

They had both since showered and changed from their daytime clothes: he was now wearing cotton slacks and a shirt and she was wearing a white vest top and a simple sarong wrapped around her waist.

Quite lovely, he thought. Again, he remembered what she had said about her ex's behaviour and could not make sense of it.

What an idiot...

"Each one is different, like a snowflake or a fingerprint," Olivia was saying about the sunset.

He glanced at her and smiled. "They are. I never thought about it but you are right. I guess with the sunset it all depends on atmospheric conditions and things like that but I prefer to think of it as a daily gift from the earth and the sun to those of us trapped in the gravity, unable to fly to the heavens," he said. Sunsets made him whimsical. Olivia made him want to sound romantic.

"You just made that up, didn't you?" she grinned.

"Yep."

"Well it was beautiful, thank you," she said and sipped her wine looking back out at the water.

"You are welcome. Whimsy keeps the world turning I think. As does romance."

They sipped their wine in silence for a moment, appreciating the way the moonlight changed with the movement of the waves.

"So Ben, have you ever been in love?" Olivia asked out of nowhere, and then looked startled as if she'd been thinking out loud.

He laughed at the look on her face.

"Sorry. That was one of those; the mouth moves faster than the brain episodes," she admitted.

He laughed at this description. "It is a fair question. Would you believe I was married at the tender age of eighteen? We were so in love," he said truthfully.

"What happened?" she asked.

"After two years we weren't anymore. Fortunately, we knew it before we brought kids into it. I would have been a crappy father anyway," he added, without remorse or rancour in his tone.

Olivia appeared to think about this and then finished

her glass of wine. He offered her the bottle and she poured another, topping his up too.

"You know, I think as bad as Derek the Dick was, I am glad it all happened before the wedding, not after the vows and paperwork and all that," she said sounding thoughtful.

"Derek the dick huh? Figures. I was thinking he must have been some kind of idiot to mess that up. You are better off without him, Olivia. Like you said, better to find that crap out before you got married." He was trying to keep a little bit of humour in his voice because he was sure it had been a heart-rending experience for her.

She just nodded. "I am trying to think about it that way - now. For a while, I thought I had to have done something wrong to have that happen to me. I just couldn't figure out what," she continued.

He shook his head, feeling incredibly protective of her. "No, it was nothing to do with you and everything to do with the guy, who really does sound like a dick. And also, it seems to me the one I might also be mad at in a situation like that would be your so-called best friend?"

She smiled slightly and nodded.

"I was for a while. She had been a friend since my early years and I will never understand what got into her. Nor do I care at this point. This whole trip is already working out better and better in that respect. Whatever her issue was, she is welcome to it. I don't want anything more to do with either of them," she finished.

"Good for you. I know it must be tough and I won't pretend to understand all that you went through. I do think you are going about it right, though. Keep busy and let time work its magic. It may not heal all wounds but it does do a good job of letting them scab over when you are not thinking about it."

Ben finished his wine and reached for the bottle again.

"That is an apt description. No wonder you are a writer. Do all writers speak so descriptively?" she asked and he could hear honest curiosity in her voice.

"Some do, some are a little leery about coming across as too bookish. For me though, I am a writer and don't feel like hiding it. People can take me or leave me. I am glad you seem to like it though. I would hate to think I was getting on your nerves all the time. It would make the lodging situation even more awkward," he said chuckling.

They both laughed in the comfortable way of people who both knew that their situation wasn't the least bit awkward at all.

Quite the opposite.

CHAPTER EIGHTEEN

*E*arly the following morning, Olivia came out of her bedroom, wrapping her robe around her.

She could hear Ben on the phone in his room and the door was shut. She could not hear what he was saying, but he did not sound happy about it.

She went along and got some coffee he had made earlier, then went out on the veranda, shutting the sliding doors behind her.

She sipped her coffee and watched the moonlight twinkling on the surf in the darkness before the sun came up. It was almost as pretty as the night before.

Mornings and evenings on the veranda were a blessing of the cottage and with only a couple of mornings left, Olivia did not want to waste these precious opportunities.

After a few minutes, the door opened behind her.

"Morning Olivia," Ben said.

"Morning. Early business?" she asked curious as to why he would be on the phone before daylight.

"My agent called. If I could reach through the phone and flip her off I would have. My Greek publisher heard I am here and they are clamouring for some PR plus a meet and greet. Seems it would go a long way to opening my books up to a new audience, at least that is what I was told," he said and took a drink of his coffee. She could see the annoyance in his eyes.

"How would that open up the market for your books?" she asked reasonably.

"My US publishers are hoping to have the new one translated into Greek also. If I do this and make a big deal of the fact that I've written it here, it may help in that direction," he explained.

"I see. I guess that makes sense. When do they want you?" she asked.

"Today apparently, I'm leaving for Athens in an hour. It is highly irritating in the middle of a perfect workflow," he said.

She shrugged. "Well, from what I have heard, part of being a writer is not only in the writing but also in other people reading it, yes?"

He nodded but still didn't look too happy.

"I guess I should go. I'm also sorry to be missing one of

your last few days here too. Can I maybe meet you for dinner at Hali's around seven?" he asked hopefully and Olivia smiled, realising at once that he seemed genuinely disappointed they wouldn't get to spend more time together.

But was it more than that? Could Ben be… interested in her? Or was he just being a good friend?

Before she could think too much more about it, he rushed off to get ready and make sure she had enough time to shower before her yoga class.

Even in his haste, Ben was thinking of her. He was a good guy and again, so utterly different to Derek it was incredible.

But felt wonderful.

CHAPTER NINETEEN

When she finished yoga class, Olivia went to breakfast and had a big plate of pancakes, Greek style. The meal was hugely filling and she felt like she was waddling to her hammock.

She decided to let it all settle a bit before lying back to snooze, so she checked the time in London and called her aunt.

"Hello darling, I hope everything is still working out OK with the double booking. Again, I am so sorry about that. I am milking it for everything I can from the management company though," Carole told her.

"All is well and we are milking it too. We have hardly had to pay for anything. It is working out great. Ben really is a nice guy - he just spends his days typing away while I am out and about. It works out fine. I just wanted to check in and see how you are doing," she told her.

"I am fine dear, and all the better now that I know all is working out. I thought it might be since I had not heard from you since. Are you having a good time otherwise?" Carole asked eagerly.

"I truly am and I owe you for this. This place is amazing, well you know that yourself. I am surprised you don't try and find a way to live here," she said, and Carole laughed.

"I thought about it but I would miss London too much. You might move there day, though," she said encouragingly.

"I am an accountant, Carole, I won't be buying a house on the cliffs of Santorini any time soon," Olivia joked and drank some lemon water.

"You never know, love. I am glad to hear you sound so good though. It sounds like the island is really working its magic on you and I am so happy about that. How are you feeling?" Olivia knew she was not asking if she had the flu.

"I am much better. Santorini is working its magic. Derek the Dick can go jump off a cliff for all I care. Actually, I am glad this whole thing happened when it did. As Ben pointed out, better before the wedding than after," she mumbled.

"You told your roommate about it?" Her aunt sounded surprised.

"Well, it is a small house. He is a nice guy, Carole. We're friends. He told me about his divorce if it helps any," she said and Carole laughed.

"I was just surprised I suppose. You can talk to whomever you want; you are a grown woman. I am glad you are making friends and it sounds like you are hooked on yoga too. Good for you, branching out. I am so proud of you and I hope the rest of your time there is as fun as it has been so far."

Olivia smiled, glad she had called her.

"Thanks and I hope all continues well with you. I have nap time scheduled on my hammock now and I don't want to keep you," she said.

"Okay darling, I will talk to you when you get back but until then, brilliant to hear from you," she said.

Olivia bid her beloved aunt goodbye and they both hung up.

Smiling she leaned back in her hammock and closed her eyes, feeling content.

It was not long before she fell asleep.

In her dreams she was rocking in a hammock with Ben laughing about something, she did not know what.

All Olivia knew was that she was incredibly happy and Derek the Dick was but a distant memory.

CHAPTER TWENTY

*a*fter her nap, time seemed to drag.

She walked the beach but couldn't find anything that sounded fun to do. About mid-afternoon she realised if Ben was not getting back until late, Hali's might be full.

She moved further up the hill away from the sound of the surf and called the restaurant.

"Hi, I was wondering if you took reservations for tables?" she asked the man on the phone.

"Of course. When would you like it for," he asked.

"Great, I was thinking about seven-thirty this evening. The little table by the olive tree near the beach, would that one be available?" she asked hopefully.

"Ah of course. Your table will be ready for you at

seven. Is there anything else I can help you with?" he asked politely.

"That will be it. Thank you for your help," she told him.

She was glad she'd thought of it. It would have been a pain to meet Ben there tonight and be unable to get a seat. She sighed and looked around the beach.

The sparkling blue water looked inviting and Olivia decided it was time for a swim.

Wading out into the water felt good and she swam around for a while, but all too quickly it seemed that too lost its excitement for her.

She trudged back up the beach, laid her towel out and stretched out on it to dry off and get some sun.

After about an hour she then got up and went to the little shower stands to shower off after swimming. She had not used them before and found them quite handy. She rinsed off the seawater and combed out her hair, letting her one-piece bathing suit dry in the sun while she put on jean shorts and a vest.

Olivia strolled back down the town, then stopped at a deli and got a Danish with a coffee. She sat under an awning and people watched for another hour before heading down the beach again.

She was feeling fretful and restless today and she did not know why.

It was weird and she wondered if she was coming down with something. She didn't feel sick, just out of sorts.

She sighed and found a bench higher up on the beach, pulled out a book and read for an hour, and found that she enjoyed just sitting and reading. Perhaps that was her problem.

She had been going non-stop since she got here, always exploring or looking for something to do other than the hammock nap, she hadn't really just idled around, doing nothing in particular.

It was about five o'clock then, and she walked up to the little bar down from Hali's, ordered wine and pulled out her book.

It was a historical mystery Ben had recommended that she was finding very engaging.

She read until almost six-thirty and then realised she should go down to Hali's to check on the reservation.

As she approached the taverna she saw the young man who had bumped into her chair that first night. He was leaving with two women on his arm and smiled mischievously at her as she passed. He was a busy boy, she thought humorously.

Then she saw Ben strolling up the beach and her smile widened. Olivia picked up the pace to meet him halfway. He was smiling too.

"Hey Ben, did you have a nice meet and greet, or whatever it was?" she asked and he laughed. He was looking a little tense, but now he seemed to visibly relax.

"It was okay. Thankfully most of the people I met spoke some English or it would have been all through translators. How has your day been?" he asked as they walked back towards Hali's.

"Good. I kept it a little slow today. Enjoyed just idling around. Missed you though."

And that was it, she realised suddenly, feeling a little embarrassed. That was why she'd been so unsettled today.

She'd been missing Ben.

He laughed and gave her a one-armed hug, obviously not in the least bit discomfited or embarrassed about her admission.

"Hungry?" he asked, as they entered the taverna and Ramone the waiter gestured them to the table. If she hadn't reserved it, they would not have had a table at all and she was doubly glad for the forethought.

They ordered some wine, and after the usual study of the menu, they ordered dinner and leaned back to relax.

Olivia immediately felt better and more relaxed than she'd been all day. Ben offered up a toast to a good evening and she returned it eagerly, lifting her glass to his, wondering how she was going to feel the day after tomorrow when her trip came to an end and she wouldn't see him ever again.

Was she falling for Ben?

CHAPTER TWENTY-ONE

*J*ust then, the food arrived and Olivia couldn't think about it any longer. She had chosen the broiled fish and he had gone with the lamb stew. They were both trying what the other had eaten the last time here. They laughed over that, as they did everything lately, and dug into the food.

It was the usual excellent quality they had become used to. She told him about swimming and walking the beach and he went over his day with her.

His sounded a lot more exciting, if a little frustrating.

"So after the short flight to Athens, I waited for two hours before seeing the publicity manager who had wanted me to come. Now as you know, I have certain ... tendencies when I don't eat. I can get a little cranky. I managed to hold it together for the guy, signed a few books and did some press, but by the time lunchtime came and went I was seriously thinking of letting my sarcasm loose on him. Fortunately, I had some time before the meet and greet with the publishers so I snuck off and went to a nearby café and ate the first thing on the menu. Would you believe it; it was a good old-fashioned American hamburger," he said with a laugh.

"A hamburger in a Greek café?" Olivia chuckled.

"I know, right? It didn't occur to me it was odd until I was halfway through. It was not jazzed up Greek style or anything. Just your typical bacon cheeseburger and it was delicious. After I stuffed my face I asked the waiter and he said it was on the menu for shy tourists who have not experienced the greatness of Greek cuisine. Or something like that. He did not speak English well and of course, I don't speak Greek at all. Anyway, after that I went back to the conference building and the handlers were freaking out. I guess I was supposed to stay out and they had lost me. I apologised and pointed out that no one had told me not to go anywhere, or even that I had handlers. They saw how that could create some confusion and accepted my apology. Then I met with about thirty people and took pictures and signed books for an hour or so. When I left everyone seemed happy. So overall it was a productive day in that sense. I would have preferred doing more exploring with you, but life does intrude sometimes," he finished and then forked up the last of his thick stew.

Olivia was laughing. "So I will keep in mind that if you ever get cranky with me, all I need to do is suggest a restaurant," she joked, and he chuckled and squeezed her hand, sending a flood of warmth from her head to the tips of her toes.

"Already you know me so well."

As they finished up and left the restaurant there was a commotion on the beach about a half mile down.

It looked like some people were setting up some kind of display, but as they got closer Olivia and Ben realised there was a group of hot air balloonists setting up multi-coloured balloons with baskets for passengers.

"The experience of a lifetime!" the Greek hawker intoned. "Consider the views of the caldera and volcano at dusk from above. Consider the peace to be found in a higher elevation alongside with the birds," he continued.

A dubious-looking tourist stepped up. "Doesn't the wind off the water make it hard to fly the things?" he asked.

"Good question," Ben murmured and Olivia giggled.

"Ah my good man, you are most observant. You have no doubt also seen how once the sun goes down, the air currents cool and the wind dies off. That is why for a beach takeoff, we wait until dusk. The amazing coincidence is that it also makes for a much more romantic trip for you and your loved one, eh?" The persuasive Greek grinned as he said this along with a sweeping, grand gesture. He was going for the hard sell.

"Not a bad pitch actually. He may even be right about the breezes at night. They do calm down," Olivia commented to Ben.

"Yeah, I wouldn't mind trying it some night. I wonder if they are going to be around for long," he mused, then stepped forward to the eager balloon trip salesman. "Excuse me, sir. Will you be here tomorrow night?" he asked.

"Of course, we are here for five more nights to serve your romantic holiday needs," he said smiling at Olivia, who could not help laughing a little. The guy was pushing it.

"Thanks, I may be back some night," Ben told the man and stepped back alongside Olivia. "It could be fun, but not tonight? I would rather have a glass on our veranda."

She nodded, pleased at how easily he had referred to it as 'our veranda'.

"Sounds like a good end to the day. Besides, we will have a front-row seat for these taking off. See how well they do before risking it," she pointed out logically.

He grinned. "Nice thinking. Do we need to stop off to pick up some wine first?"

CHAPTER TWENTY-TWO

They headed off and by the time sunset had begun Ben and Olivia were back on the veranda with a glass and some cookies to munch on.

As usual, they stood together at the railing to watch the sunset.

Olivia noticed that again, this one was different from the previous nights. Instead of covering the horizon or a straight line downward, the glorious red and orange hues seemed to come off the water in majestic star patterns that took her breath away.

She and Ben watched in silence as the patterns brightened, glaring and beautiful and then slowly faded over several minutes until it was gone.

"Oh, look they are going to start filling the balloons. I am glad they waited, the flames would have been a distraction," he said pointing to the beach below and to the right twenty yards or so.

He was right. They watched men and women with flashlights setting up the furnaces that would fill the balloons and then fire them up. The whooshing sound of the furnace was powerful and seemed to echo up from the beach. It created a dramatic atmosphere as they watched, sipping their wine.

"I bet that is loud as hell in the basket when they are flying," Ben said.

"I hadn't thought of that, but you are right. Then again once you are up it is more a matter of them just blasting it now and then. I watched them fly out of Edinburgh once. It wasn't at night though, this should be good," she said.

Ben nodded in agreement then grabbed a few cookies and handed her one. She nibbled on the chocolate and sipped her wine as one by one, the balloons filled slowly, like the stirring of a long-sleeping dragon.

The breeze had died down to almost nothing, and sure enough, they got to watch each one take off with two passengers per ride.

It was an amazing sight and Olivia was glad they had not rushed to try it without watching it first. Each balloon was different and beautiful in its own way.

The first to go up was dark except for star-shaped

patterns that were clear and let the light from the furnace shine through.

As it took off each burst of the furnace lit up the star patterns in the night sky and it floated up right in front of their balcony, then slowly took off down the beach from a few hundred feet in the air.

The second had a giant butterfly pattern, one on each side, so shaped that the wings looked like thinly veined delicate wings that again lit up with every burst of the balloon's furnace.

The crowd on the beach cheered and they could hear shouts from the balloon's passengers too. The last one was dark with pinpoints, like stars in the sky all over its surface. So it looked like a globe of stars as it rose and then followed the other two down the beach.

Olivia and Ben watched them all until they were out of sight and she sighed contentedly as they sat back down.

Ben poured them both another glass of wine.

"That was amazing. First the sunset, and then the majesty of the balloons. I am not sure if I want to take a ride and miss watching the take offs though. I have never seen balloons take flight before, it is amazing," he said, still memorised by the experience.

"I know what you mean. I did watch them in Scotland, but in daylight. They were still beautiful, but nothing like this. Santorini is still full of surprises, isn't it? I am glad we got to see it," she said.

But Olivia was especially glad she got to witness it with Ben. She thought briefly that Derek would have talked through the whole thing, as was his way, spoiling it.

Ben was head and shoulders a better man than her ex.

Neither of them had spoken while it was happening, but having a companion seemed to make the experience all the more special. That and the sunsets were something they'd shared together.

Indeed this whole trip was becoming a shared experience, and all the better for it, Olivia realised.

Ben's dark eyes glinted in the little lights they had on the table between them.

"Isn't this just the perfect spot to end a day?" he said as if reading her mind. "Two of us sharing our day's adventures with a glass of wine and an amazing view."

Olivia couldn't be sure, but she thought he was looking at her when he said the words 'amazing view'.

Then he cleared his throat and looked back out at the sea and she felt herself blush. He seemed embarrassed by the comment now, and she looked away so as not to compound his discomfort.

She knew she was being ridiculous, considering she had just come off of a bad separation, but she was attracted to Ben.

Derek was so far out of her mind right then, that there was no way this could be a rebound situation.

Ben had looked at her with more than just friendship in his eyes - she was sure of it - and she felt the same way herself when she looked at him.

Maybe it was the wine, or maybe just the fact that she was on holiday, but there and then Olivia realised something important.

She was well and truly over Derek.

CHAPTER TWENTY-THREE

*B*en woke early and immediately began writing after his first cup of coffee. He had so many ideas that it flowed quickly.

He heard Olivia's usual soft steps as she got ready and then left for her sunrise yoga.

He had thought about going along with her one of the days but decided they both needed their personal time, and yoga was a spiritual thing.

She never spoke of it beyond how much she enjoyed it.

For his part, he was glad to get another early start to the day so he could spend some more time with Olivia. They had discussed their day's plans and had decided to go shopping, purely for the fun of it.

Ben had seen an open-air market yesterday on his ride from the house to the airport and wanted to see it on foot.

She liked the idea so when the time came, he finished up the chapter he was on and got cleaned up for the day.

Today, he wore shorts and a loose shirt with sandals, unlike yesterday when he'd had to wear a suit, which he resented and made him feel like he was back in New York having boring meetings with his publishers and agent.

Santorini was amazing and he had begun to wonder if buying a place here might be a good idea. Sure, he would still have to spend some time in the Big Apple for work, but he would not mind spending the bulk of his time in such an enchanting place.

He was most definitely thinking of extending his time on Santorini in any case. Maybe even write his whole book here? With the success of his last few, it was not like he couldn't afford it. But of course, it wasn't just the island that held an attraction to him.

He realised for sure the previous day - when he'd had to spend time away from the island - that he was becoming very attached to Olivia. She was energetic, cheerful and more fun to be around than anyone he had ever met.

Not to mention that she was beautiful, funny and smart as well as compassionate.

He guessed that she had realised his attraction at one point the night before, and hoped she might feel the same, but due to her recent past with her ex, Derek the dick, he did not want to presume anything.

Still, tomorrow would be her last night and their time together was running out….

As he approached the yoga group he saw Olivia and waved.

No, he told himself, just wait and see what happens. Don't rush her.

He had no intention of destroying a perfectly good friendship.

"Breakfast and shopping then?" she smiled, coming up to him. She looked energetic and ready to go. Ben smiled back. He always smiled around her.

"Yep. I am looking forward to it. I can't imagine what sort of things the shops will have here, but I can't wait to find out."

They walked up the beach on the way for breakfast and she told him about the sunrise.

"It is a little different from our sunsets because the sun is rising behind us, over the island. It is kind of cool though, how the beach slowly lights up. Like slowly turning up the light controls in a room. Gradually getting stronger until it shines on the day," she said and he noticed that she had these cute little dimples that he had never spotted before.

They took an outside table in the shade at a nearby cafe.

"Now who is speaking like a writer?" he joked. "Lovely description, nice job."

"Thanks. Coming from a professional writer that is a compliment," she said, picking up the menu. "I must warn you, I tried the pancakes yesterday and I would advise against it unless you want to be weighed down for a few hours. I'm serious, they're great but would slow down a cheetah," she added.

"Good advice. My usual is heavy enough. I think I'll stick with the potatoes and veggie plate."

CHAPTER TWENTY-FOUR

*A*fter breakfast, they skipped the hammock nap until after the shopping and soon found themselves walking down the streets through charming cobblestone courtyards.

Most of the houses and businesses looked identical: painted the same bright white with red brick edging and tumbling bougainvillaea.

The gardens were bright and colourful and when they came upon the market square it was even brighter with banners and wafting scents of cooking food.

Olivia and Ben looked at each other with anticipation, both obviously thinking: *This is going to be fun*. He liked the idea that they were so easily able to communicate without words.

He enjoyed watching her barter too. Coming from the

States, he was used to the sticker price being what you paid for things.

Whereas Olivia had travelled enough around France and Spain to have picked up a talent for bartering. She was good, as far as he could tell, so he let her do the talking and she always brought the sellers down from their original asking price.

They mostly bought little keepsakes; Olivia picked up some things for her aunt and Ben found some wonderful hand-carved pens for his office.

He did very little handwriting anymore but he'd always preferred it to typing and had been wanting to get back into note-taking.

This trip was the first time he had done it in some time, and it was good for his creative juices, so maybe the pens would help him get even more motivated in that regard.

They finished up buying some fresh bread and a few bottles of some local wine that was recommended by a restauranteur at lunchtime. They were going to try it that evening on the veranda at their usual sunset-watching.

Walking back towards the beach with their packages in the afternoon was just as enjoyable. They greeted people they did not know and laughed at two little dogs playing in someone's garden.

Just a relaxing time with a person Ben was growing

more and more to like and respect for her easy-going adventurous spirit.

He was also becoming more and more aware of her beauty. He had always been aware of Olivia's beauty of course; he wasn't blind, but now he was catching himself looking at her more in appreciation and attraction.

Her hair was wild, and during their walk back was constantly being pushed back from her eyes.

She was wearing shorts, a vest top and a little sweater over it. It was casual, yet she wore it like a princess in a modern-day fairy tale. She caught him looking at her and smiled slightly before blushing and looking away.

That was a good sign, wasn't it?

EVENTUALLY, they made it back to the hammock place along the beach and with a sigh settled in with cocktails and the sea in front of them.

Ben now understood how this shaded little piece of the paradise around them was so attractive to Olivia.

She put her hands behind her head and closed her eyes.

He lay back too, and for a while just watched the passing tourists down on the sand.

His eyes kept going back to Olivia though, relaxing in her hammock. Her heart-shaped face was smiling slightly and her breathing was deep and even. She was the picture of health and happiness, at least in his eyes.

Beautiful and relaxed.

Just taking the day as it came with no stress or mess. She was an admirable woman and he put his own hands behind his head and closed his eyes.

Ben could still see her as he drifted off into a pleasant dream of beach adventures with his friend.

Wondering if it was becoming more.

Hoping it would.

THE TWO DOZED on longer than anticipated and realised that getting a table for dinner may be difficult.

They also still had their packages to carry up to the cottage, as well as getting changed for dinner and that would take time.

It was a dilemma, but only for a moment.

"Olivia, I wonder if Hali's deliver?" Ben asked and she grinned widely.

"That is a brilliant idea. I think they do actually, because I've seen employees rushing out with orders. I hadn't thought about that. Genius." She began digging through her purse for her phone.

"If they are willing to take an order, I will have the

same as last night," he told her. He had loved the broiled fish.

She gave him a thumbs-up as she held the phone to her ear. He listened to her talk to the staff at Hali's and order the food they wanted.

"Maybe an hour," she said into the phone, glancing at him for confirmation. He figured an hour would be good timing and nodded. They were almost back to the cottage as it was.

"Great, thanks," she finished up and then turned to Ben. "We will have it in an hour. Let's haul this stuff up and get organised," she said and picked up the pace to the path up the hill under their veranda.

Ben noticed then that she had a slight limp and wondered about it, but did not mention it. No doubt she would if it was important.

"he shower is all yours," he said when they reached the cottage. "I will put some of this stuff away and keep an eye out in case the food is early."

Ben stored the bread, stacked Olivia's purchases by her bedroom door, and then put his stuff away.

Next, he opened the wine and let it breathe.

When Olivia came back out of the bathroom she was already dressed and sent him off to the shower in turn.

By the time dinner arrived, they were both more than ready for it and shared a glass of the most excellent wine, with a name Ben could not pronounce to save his life.

They had decided that trying to spread their feast out comfortably on the small patio table would not work, so they used the table in the cottage to eat on.

It was at the window so they still had a view and a light sea breeze.

They ate hungrily and finished just in time to go out on the patio to watch the sunset and the balloons.

He noticed as they went out that she was limping a little more. He could not help but glance down at her bare foot as they stood at the balcony and Olivia noticed him looking.

"I think I twisted my ankle on a cobblestone along the market path," she told him grimacing. "The shower seemed to help, but after sitting for dinner it has begun aching. I am sure it is nothing though," she assured him.

"Are you sure? I had to spend time with a massage therapist for research once and learned all sorts of things. Apparently rubbing it and stretching the muscle helps to keep it from staying injured longer," he told her, a little nervously.

Though he did want to help, he hoped she wouldn't think the offer of a massage was weird or inappropriate.

She smiled. "Maybe I'll try it after the sunset, thanks," she said and as they turned away to watch the nightly theatre they both fell silent.

Watching the sunset together had very quickly become a pleasant, yet solemn occasion for them both. An important ritual in some way beyond the beauty of it.

Once again the display was different to the night before.

Ben watched and sipped his wine as the sun got lower and lower. He did not know if somewhere in the distance there was an atmospheric condition that was muting the usual brightness, but the red-orange color was duller, fading as the light did.

Then, just before it went out of sight it burst through in one bright brilliant blast of colour and they both gasped.

"Wow," Olivia sighed softly. He looked over at her, and she was still looking out at the water with an unreadable expression on her face.

Wow indeed, he thought, no longer thinking about the sunset.

CHAPTER TWENTY-SIX

*A*s the sun faded, they sat down for the balloon launch. Olivia bent her leg up and massaged her ankle while sitting cross-legged in her chair.

"Just trying to get some circulation back," she told him and Ben realised having her legs folded up like that was probably awkward for her to work on her ankle herself.

"I can give it a go at massaging it for you now if you'd like?" he suggested.

Olivia swivelled in her seat slightly, swinging her leg over to him.

Trying his utmost not to react to this oddly intimate situation, Ben adjusted his position with her ankle on his knee and tried to remember what he had learned from the massage therapist.

Her skin felt so soft to the touch and he gulped a little,

wondering what it would be like to run his hands all over her body.

Resisting the temptation to do just that, Ben tenderly massaged Olivia's ankle and foot as the second balloon finished filling and rose up in front of them.

As he did, they munched on some of the cookies they had gotten the day before and were still fresh.

Ben had no idea why the food on Santorini was so good but he had stopped wondering about it and just accepted it. Like so many things on this trip, he was pleasantly surprised but did not need to analyse too closely.

He just wanted to enjoy it and take in all the wonderful stimuli he could.

"So did you enjoy the shopping trip?" Olivia asked when he'd finished. "That was brilliant, thank you."

"Watching you negotiate was an education," he chuckled. "I may write some of it down tonight for future reference. This whole island feels like a fairy tale coming to life. How does your ankle feel?" he asked, as she gently rotated it herself.

Then she stood up, took a few steps and turned back with a smile.

"It does not hurt at all now. I think you did it - you're a genius," she exclaimed happily and spun in place again, before reaching over for her wine glass.

He got up too and they stood at the railing shoulder to

shoulder as the light faded, watching the people on the beach packing up their gear and going to wherever the balloons were going to land.

A little way down some people had started a beach fire.

"You know I think this book is going to be some of my best work," Ben said thoughtfully. "Something about this island, even with the summer tourists and crowds, there is something so *right* about the place that it tugs at me. Everything I have experienced has been amazing. Except maybe the lost luggage," he added and she laughed.

"I know exactly what you mean. And I'll be sorry to leave the day after tomorrow - for more reasons than one," she added, and after a beat turned to look at him.

Ben met her gaze then and out of the blue gently put his arm around her.

She did not resist, and they stood together quietly at the railing, drinking in the magnificent view and listening to the revelry on the beach.

Ben liked that it was far enough away to not be too loud, but close enough to enjoy it.

It was then that he realised that Olivia's eyes were glistening in the late evening sunlight, and she looked desperately sad.

"What is it?" he asked, dropping his arm quickly, worried now he'd come on too strong.

"It's nothing ... it's just, this trip really has been more incredible than I could ever have imagined."

"I know."

"And ... tomorrow is my last full day, and I don't want to say goodbye. To Santorini ... these wonderful sunsets ... you."

At this, she turned to face him directly, and Ben's heart soared.

Olivia had never been impulsive, not on this level but saying out loud what she was thinking just then felt so right she decided to just go with her instincts.

What she had said was true; she did not want to say goodbye to any of this, least of all Ben, whom she'd now well and truly fallen for.

"I was worried about how you were feeling, but then I felt well...maybe..." he murmured, stammering to a halt as he turned to face her and took both her hands in his.

They looked into each other's eyes and for Olivia, everything around them seemed to fade into the distance - it was just them in that moment.

Ben had a soft smile on his face as he bent his head, and their lips finally met for a delicious first kiss that was filled with promise, while all around them Santorini was bathed in a golden glow.

"I think, much like the balloons, we should just take advantage of the atmospheric conditions and see what happens," Ben said, a gentle smile on his face. "It can't hurt, can it?"

"You're absolutely right," she said, beaming back at him. "Let's just see where the wind takes us."

But balloons aside, Olivia already felt like she was floating on air, and knew that no matter what the future held, this particular Santorini sunset was one she and Ben would treasure forever.

Enjoy more Greek **Island sunshine reads from the Escape to the Islands series - available now!**

ALSO AVAILABLE

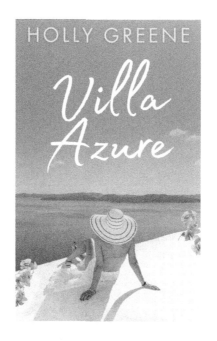

ALSO AVAILABLE

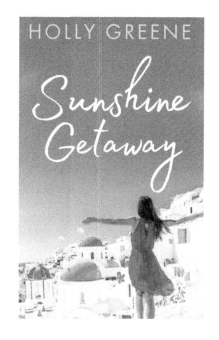

Escape to Italy Series

Escape to the Islands Series

Printed in Great Britain
by Amazon